RAVE REVIEWS FOR KATE ALLURE

LAWYER UP

"The sensuality and sexuality are palpable…**4 Stars!**"

—RT Book Reviews

"*Lawyer Up* puts the sexiness back in suits and ties (especially ties) with a collection of sizzling stories exploring how bad a person can be in the bedroom while still keeping it legal. **Best Romances of August 2016**"

—Amazon's Omnivoracious

"Discovering unexpected second chances and finding love again. Every tale is unique and pure hot perfection…Read with caution — your hands may acquire scorch marks. **5 Stars!**"

—Goodreads

"Intense chemistry, great characterization, and a kinky page-singeing ending will have readers clamoring for more…all three stories pack an emotional punch."

—Publishers Weekly

LAYING PIPE

"Seriously these two made me laugh, the playful nature, the sex rolled off the pages and Joe made Lexi feel great about herself. I loved the playful, witty dialogue. It's a quick and easy read and so light hearted. What a refreshing change to have a fun, playful book with two perfect peas in a pod. " **4 Stars!**

— Goodreads

PLAYING DOCTOR

"Kate Allure deals in pure fantasy, a spirited diversion from the mundane and a chance to explore some of the most titillating "what ifs" readers can imagine."

—*RT Book Reviews*

"Readers will cheer on these strong women as they take the initiative, seeking (and finding) both sexual satisfaction and emotional fulfillment."

—*Publishers Weekly*

"Fun, flirty characters abound, and there's plenty of kinky action."

— *Library Journal*

"This book was smoking Hot! Being a nurse I can say I loved this theme because there are a lot of hot doctors and interns out there that you can't help but fantasize about…"

—*Goodreads Bookaholic GE*

BED & BREAKFAST & BONDAGE

"Hotter than a steam room on a hot summer's day. Yeah that probably didn't make sense but when you read this book you will be craving the ice cubes for the cool down that surely won't come even as the last word is read."

—*Amazon Customer Review*

"Very sexy but with strong characters. Suspenseful where I was even worried about the bad guy…It's fun and entertaining."

—*The Booksage*

Bed & Breakfast
& BONDAGE

KATE ALLURE

ISBN: 978-1-7326957-1-9
Published 2018 by Kate Allure Books
Cover Design by Steven Glapa

KateAllure.com

Bed & Breakfast
& BONDAGE

Chapter 1

~ just outside the Napa Valley town of St. Helena

"Hey…knock, knock. Can I come in?"

The deeply masculine voice was accompanied by rapping on the frame of the ajar door to the old fieldstone shed.

Cat looked down from her perch high on a ladder. "Sure, Mason. I'm up here."

Steele Plumbing's young sexy owner sauntered in, work vest slung over his shoulder and hanging by a finger. "Just want to gather my tools, sweet thang, before I head out."

Mason bent down to grab a crescent wrench from among the items scattered about the stone floor, giving her a fine view of his *very* fine backside. He tossed the wrench into his open toolkit and reached for a screwdriver.

Cat pretended to keep working on hanging the sumptuous velvet curtains while surreptitiously watching the oh-so f-ing good-looking plumber. He wore his usual threads—sturdy boots, slightly beat-up jeans, and a faded t-shirt that stretched around his chiseled pecs and thick biceps. Mason had ditched his sturdy vest earlier on this sweltering September day, making Cat wish her top could come off too. Now the view of his tight ass in those skintight jeans made her feel like a cat in heat on a hot tin roof.

Meow-za!

Only problem—the roof on her hundred-year-old wine house was slate and the only reason she was in heat was due to her self-imposed exile from sex.

Nevertheless…

Man! He was a hot specimen.

She waited a beat…and there it was, the unwanted but all too familiar reaction to a man who was nothing more than a contractor on her remodel project. Her body kicked into high gear—her tits tightening and palms moistening and other parts moistening too. Cat ignored it, pretending it wasn't so, just as she'd done over the endless two months he'd worked on her property. It was ridiculous, really. In her recently-abandoned life down in the City of Angels, she'd spent many, *many* nights in sex clubs where gorgeous men, straight or gay, often went starkers. She'd always looked her fill, sometimes had even been granted leave to do more than look. There was no reason for her body to act this way over one guy.

She sighed.

"Got a minute?" the man of her thoughts asked.

Startled from her waking dream, Cat felt her face flush as she realized Mason had been watching her watch him, the burgundy curtains clutched, forgotten, in her hands. He stood at the bottom of the ladder grinning, obviously enjoying the view of her backside in tiny shorts.

"Um. Sure. What can I do for you?"

"Well for starters you can concede that we're made for each other and finally accept my invitation to dinner. That's what you can do for me, sweet thang." His voice was as hot and steamy as sin and straight out of Satan's love grotto.

He climbed onto the bottom rung of the ladder, his face now within kissing distance of the back of her thighs. "What d'ya say? I promise, cross my love-struck heart, that I'll show you a good time and the best wine and chow St. Helena has to offer. Afterwards, well, I'll show you an *even* better time...*Fernball*."

"I wish now I'd never told you my middle name." But she smiled at his joke anyway. The gorgeous man knew perfectly well she preferred Cat to his silly tease on her middle name. She also wished her mom's favorite childhood book hadn't been *Charlotte's Web*. However, she'd learned that correcting Mason was a waste of time, and, anyway, she kind of liked the sexy way he purred it.

Mason smirked at her, a challenge in his hazel green eyes.

Suddenly, Cat needed to give it right back to him, forgetting her desire to keep everything professional between them. Staring down at Mason, she matched him grin for grin. "So, Mr. Steele, tell me what's the title of your best flick?"

"Huh?" He dropped down and took a step back to see her face.

"I want to watch you in action."

"Still don't know what you're talking about, sweet thang." Confusion wrinkled his brow and drew his lips together into a sort of cute masculine pout that made Cat want to plant a big one right there.

"You've got a name fit for a porn star. I can see the movie title on the billboard now." She gestured broadly with the hand that wasn't gripping the tall ladder and threw his words back at him. "*I'll Show You a Good Time*, starring Mason Steele, and featuring his stone-hard pecs and sturdy buns of steel." She looked pointedly down at his assets. "You'd make a mint."

His confusion drained away. "Yeah, yeah. I've heard it all before."

But then Mason smirked and quirked an eyebrow. "Like what you see?"

He swiveled in place while flexing those oh so hard pectorals. Giving her his backside and watching over his shoulder, he vogued like a Hollywood stripper. "Got lots more to show you for the right incentive." Mason's grin was pure sex as he began to twerk his firm ass for her benefit.

"Wait right there," she ordered, laughing.

Ogling him, she started down the ladder, one hand holding on and the other digging into her tiny back pocket. "Strippers expect tips and I've got…"

Her hand came up empty. "Shoot."

Still rushing down the ladder, she rummaged in her other back pocket, letting go of the rung for a split second. "I know I've got some money—"

"Stop! Cat."

She missed a step, and her hand fumbled to grasp thin air. She careened backwards, arms flailing, and fell through the air…

And into Mason's sturdy grasp. He anchored her tightly against his body. "I've got you," he soothed, his husky voice as sweet and thick as warm maple syrup. He didn't immediately lower her to the stone floor, his cheek nuzzling her hair. His breath tingled her neck like dancing butterflies on her sensitive skin. She sensed Mason was as lost in her as she was in him.

Motionless, Cat was caught in a sensual cocoon, unable to resist his six feet of solid male yumminess. She leaned into him, letting the moment stretch, wanting the pleasure, the connection. Wanting him.

Mason didn't know it, but all it would take was a certain tone in his voice—commanding, not requesting—and she would drop her panties for him...or drop to kneel at his feet. Whatever he wanted, she'd be helpless to stop herself from obeying him.

In a way, her uncontrollable reaction to him was annoying. Mason wasn't that kind of lover, she was sure of it. He was a nice guy and nice guys didn't do it for her in the bedroom. There was no hope for them having a lasting relationship, which was why she never accepted his many invitations.

Cat doubted that she'd be as affected by him, if it weren't for her real problem. It had been too damn long since she'd felt a man's body against hers. Only a few months really, but still...too...damn...long! At least, that's what she told herself.

Cat nudged his ribs with her elbow. "Mason, you can let go now."

He released her as swiftly as a cat would leap from hot bricks. She dropped the last few inches to the ground, landing on all twos. Rotating quickly, she faced him, wanting to see if he looked like she felt—oddly bereft and dangerously needy, like the place that she really belonged was right back in his arms. But Mason had turned away and was putting distance between them even as she wanted to call him back.

From across the nearly empty space, he turned to face her. They stared at each other, both breathing heavily. The atmosphere in the dark, hundred-year-old stone shed became charged with tension, a shadowy, not quite sinister aura that to Cat always meant sex. The wine house, now hung with thick velvet drapes, was on its way to becoming the perfect dungeon, but the renovation was not for him. She was not for him. He would never understand her dark desires, and while Cat vowed she'd never again feel shame about her need for kink, she wouldn't go out of her way to seek ridicule either. She needed to put this whatever-it-was between them where it belonged—behind a facade of professionalism. Impersonal. Sterile. Platonic.

Clearing her throat, Cat drew herself up—all five feet, eight inches of feisty femininity—to meet his hungry eyes with firm but friendly detachment. "Thank you for the rescue. I've got quite a bit of work to finish today, and I'm sure you're busy too. So where are we on finishing up and getting the inspector out in time for my grand opening three weeks from now?"

He winced at her formal tone, but Mason responded like the professional he was. "We're in great shape. Nearly everything's done, with the one exception of the tub. The manufacturer went bust, so I've found you two alternatives. Unfortunately they both cost thirty percent more."

He walked to where the luxury claw-foot tub would go, not in the small bathroom that housed only a toilet and sink, but right in the middle of the big open room that once housed barrels of fermenting wine for the small vineyard that no longer existed. The large glass-walled shower with double showerheads was already installed nearby, waiting for guests, but he didn't know that.

"This space is going to make a terrific art studio," Mason noted, studying it. He pointed to the thick, black padding that now lined the ceiling. "What's that? Looks like sound insulation."

Cat had recently discovered that the tile roof didn't block sound nearly as well as the thick stone walls, so she'd hired someone to fix the problem and had prepared an explanation for it as well. "Metal work can be quite loud, and I don't want the B&B guests to be disturbed at night."

Cat watched as his eyes caught on the industrial-strength metal hooks installed in the ceiling crossbeams—work she'd also hired elsewhere. She regretted lying to him every time, but the building's true purpose had to remain a secret. Only her peeps from L.A. knew the truth, and they would be up in three weeks to install fixtures and set up equipment. If Mason asked, Cat wondered whether she should tell him it was none of his business or give him her fake giant mobile answer.

Or, maybe, tell him the whole fucking truth.

Not likely.

She held her breath when Mason looked back at her, seeming to weigh his words. "Well, I just want to throw it out there…I've been impressed with how much hard work you've put in to save money. I know you're on a tight budget and the rotted plumbing that we had to replace in the farmhouse pinched your budget even more. So here's an idea. How about you forgo the tub altogether or maybe install it later when money is not as tight."

"You've clearly given it some thought and I appreciate that, but I feel my…art studio won't be right without it. Artists are quirky, you know." She flashed him a small smile and shrugged.

"I can understand wanting to make this space conducive to spurring your creative juices, but this would save you a couple grand."

Cat held back her snort of laughter. Yes, there'd be juices flowing and copious creativity, but not of the kind he was thinking. She felt her lips tilt up at her secret witticism.

Mason gave her a funny look but said only, "You're the boss."

He turned and headed toward the arched wood door. It was the original—thick weathered oak with iron band hinges. She had hated marring it with the installation of a high-tech, push-code lock, but security would be crucial for her and her guests.

Mason paused in the doorway. "Did I see two dogs peering out of the main farmhouse when I drove up?"

"Yes. I just adopted a pair of fantastic and fantastically huge mutts. They guard-dogged a farm in Cottonwood before the elderly lady sold out and moved to be near her daughter in the south bay."

"I'm pleased to know you'll be safe out here alone. Not that St. Helena isn't safe," he was quick to add, "but with all your artwork and stuff, you can't be too careful and I'd hate it if anything bad ever happened to you."

His earnest tone and sincere expression told her Mason really meant it, and that warmed her heart. Cat moved toward him, wanting a physical connection again, even though she knew she'd never act on the desire. "Thank you for suggesting I get a guard dog. That was a primo idea."

"My pleasure, as always...*Fernball.*" With a grin and a mock salute he left her, striding to his truck with his tool-belt-swinging swagger, which she'd already memorized in fine detail.

Mason waved as he climbed inside, calling, "One way or another, I promise to get all the work done by the inspector's arrival."

Cat returned his friendly gesture and watched from the doorway as he drove down the long driveway back toward St. Helena's main drag.

She pulled shut the heavy door, but the place was too quiet now. It missed his cocky, outsized presence.

Soon the wine house would be finished, ready for renting to a select word-of-mouth clientele. From then on, she'd never let Mason back inside to discover her true nature, never wanting to see his shock and disapproval. Fighting an unwarranted letdown—he was nothing to her but a contracted plumber—she closed the place and punched in the code on the lock, before walking back to the main house.

Cat took a long hot shower in the master suite. Might as well enjoy the luxury herself before she had guests, she decided. Closing her eyes, she let the water wash away her worries along with the sweat and dirt from the day's remodeling work. Without conscious thought, Cat found herself leaning against the wall, the high-end rain shower pouring on her like a waterfall as her mind wandered back to that moment when Mason had his arms around her. He had radiated masculinity and strength.

What would have happened if she hadn't nudged Mason with her elbow? He always seemed ready to play with his overblown flirting and cocky grin. She imagined his large capable hands, a workman's hands, sliding over her body as the warm rivulets of water caressed her skin. She shivered remembering his hot breath on the curve of her neck.

Losing herself in a sensual haze, Cat could almost feel his lips teasing her skin, trailing kisses along the ridge of her shoulder and down until his hot mouth latched onto one of her breasts. Her core tightened right along with the peaking of her nipples. He'd be a hot, demanding lover, instinct told her—not a trained Dom of course, but still ferocious. Her pussy clenched, the sharp desire almost uncomfortable. Cat's eyes popped open.

"Stop this." She was currently without a Dom or even a lover and likely to remain that way for a long while. Fantasizing about a guy she could never have—not for more than a quick fling anyway—was self-defeating. Worse. It would turn a pleasant itch into raging lust. Cat switched off the shower and grabbed a towel.

"Forget about him," she mumbled. "Stay focused on what matters." And that was to make the B&B a smashing success and pay off her debt.

Before going up to her private bedroom and office suite, converted from a dusty attic, Cat put a red X across one more day on her big project calendar hanging on the refrigerator. *Thank god I'm almost done!*

Even though she'd padded both the budget and the timeline, unexpected developments had eaten away all her surplus funds, so it was doubly important that nothing else slip. Soon, she'd be her own businessperson. Even more important, with reservations starting to flow in, she'd be able to begin paying down the money she'd borrowed to cover the farmhouse remodel.

Grabbing some cold pizza and a glass of wine, Cat climbed two flights to the attic. The appellation from historic Alfonis Winery was delicious. She recorded the vintage and brand in the notebook she'd been using while she sampled all of St. Helena's finest. Munching her dinner, she worked on the marketing campaign and website for Tulip House until her eyes started to blur.

Cat turned off the lights, and the bright moonlight shining in through the old, round, dormer window drew her forward. Staring down at the grey landscape to the wine house farther back on her property, she wondered if that part of the business plan would really work. Could she manage to keep it a secret and rent it out at the same time? Her success depended on that extra income. But what would happen if the good people of St. Helena found out what was really going on inside the old shed. Could they revoke her B&B license?

Her phone buzzed and she hurried to pick it up. When she saw who was calling, her stomach knotted. Cat wished he would leave her alone, and it took effort to sound appropriately pleasant and happy to hear from him. "Good evening, Master Lynch."

"How is *my* Pussycat tonight?" His magnificent voice was just like the magnificent man—dark, modulated, cultured. But it was the possessiveness in his tone that made Cat want to claw herself free.

She adopted a bright, happy tone, hoping to reassure him that the project was good so she could end the call quickly. "Working hard, Sir. I'm pleased to report that the remodel is almost finished. I'm sure I'll be able to make my first payment to you right on time."

"Great. Good to hear." But he'd spit the words out as if they tasted of sour milk. "Since you're in such good shape, I'd like you to come back home for a visit. Lynchland isn't the same without you, and I miss my favorite pussy. Don't you miss me too?"

A rancid taste now flooded Cat's mouth, and she had to work to draw him off the scent. "Of course, Sir, I miss everyone down in L.A., and you've been such a big part of my life for so long. How could I not miss you?" Cat hoped he'd let that slide and not press her.

"So you'll come home next weekend?"

Cat took a deep breath. "Sir, I'll always remember our time together, fondly, and everything I learned from you, but St. Helena is my home now."

"You're still my submissive. I haven't released you and won't so long as the contracts are in place, agreements you willingly signed."

"I know, Sir. I'll pay you back the money, I promise."

"And the second contract?"

"I'll honor that one too, if need be, but for now I just can't leave the B&B. The opening is just a couple weeks away, and I still need to set up the wine house. But I hope you know that I'm so grateful to you for your support, and I want you to be proud of me."

"I am proud, but you don't have to do it all yourself. That's too much stress for you. I want you to hire a contractor for that, and let me work out your stress in the way that you love. The more I think about it, the more I insist you take a break."

"I just can't!" she squawked.

Shit. Shit. Shit.

Cat clenched the cellphone in a death grip as an all too familiar feeling—a mix of claustrophobia and panic—scratched at her like thorns in a briar patch. Would she ever be free of this man?

Cat sucked a quick breath, then modulated her voice to the dusky song of a siren. The sound Lynch preferred. "Sir," she purred. "I'm ever so grateful for your thoughtfulness, but I've got it covered. Gotham and Sady and their subs are coming up in three weeks to help set up the dungeon. They're bringing everything. So you don't have to worry about me."

"You invited your friends up for a visit." Lynch said it without inflection. Flat. Toneless. And Cat knew she'd really screwed up.

"It's not for play. We're going to work all weekend. That's why I didn't invite you. Of course, I'd value your input but I know how busy you are."

"For you, my dear sweet Pussy, I'll make the time."

"But you're the master. It's so below your—"

"Nonsense. I've wanted to check up on my investment. And on you. It seems you need a little maintenance to help you remember what it is to be a sub, *my* sub. I'll see you in three weeks."

He hung up before she could stop him, not that she had any idea how to object to her Dom visiting his submissive and his investment. Cat had known for a while that she needed a clean break from Master Lynch, but then she'd gone and done the opposite, cementing herself to him by accepting his loan for her business. She stared down at the wine house, the center of her plan to turn this property she'd inherited into a thriving B&B and private luxury dungeon. It was her escape from Lynch and her chance for a new future, but there were still obstacles to overcome.

It will all work out. It has to!

Cat promised herself that she'd not stop trying until she made her business a huge success, and then she could pay off the loans and turn in her collar.

And then, finally, she'd truly be free of her past.

Chapter 2

~ one week later, late afternoon

Mason stood back to look at the finished product. A brand new claw-foot tub big enough for two stood on the flagstone floor, ready to use. He started to gather his tools, but, as always, his thoughts were squarely on the alleged artist and future proprietress, Catriona Fern Morrison.

Everything about her intrigued him. She had a springtime-fresh innocence that seemed at odds with the sultry vixen he caught glimpses of at times. He bet she'd be amazing in the sack, sex-pistol one minute and sweet surrender the next. But there was more to her than that. Cat had a quiet drive and strong work ethic—something he shared and admired in others. At the same time, she seemed to have a free-spirited enthusiasm for life. He could use a little more of that in his own daily existence. He rarely let go and enjoyed himself, to focused on building his business.

The massive tub was just one more example of her mixing work and play. He thought it odd that she wanted it placed out in the middle of the studio, rather than in the back corner next to the shower, but now he could see how utterly decadent and inviting it looked there.

Soon, maybe even tonight, Cat would soak in it. Naked. With bubbles. He just knew there'd be bubbles. They would mostly hide her but also offer tantalizing glimpses of bare flesh. Her sexy breasts, not too big but firm round handfuls, would be swathed in frothy suds, her nipples, teasing pink buds, peeking through. His mouth watered. He would slide in behind her and settle her slick softness against his hard front, nestling her ass at his crotch.

A rush of lust like a locomotive bearing down just about knocked him to his knees. His jeans bulged, tight and uncomfortable. His hand flexed with need to finish the fantasy.

"Shit!" His frustration bounced off the bare stone walls.

Mason turned away and grabbed another tool off the floor, willing his hard-on to oblivion. This fantasy wasn't going to happen, ever, not if Cat kept turning down his dinner invitations. He wished that just one time she'd accept, give him a chance to show her that he was a good guy. There was something that made her hesitate. She had secrets. He was sure of it, and that made her all the more interesting. She wasn't attached—had admitted to him that she wasn't involved with anyone.

No, wait.

He paused, wrench in hand, that wasn't what she'd said. Her exact words had been, "I don't belong to any man." What a weird thing to say. Regardless, she hadn't rejected his invitations because she had a boyfriend. And it wasn't because she had a girlfriend either—not by the way she ogled his ass, his mouth, his everything, when she thought he wasn't looking.

Mason realized he hadn't exactly helped his case. Every time he was around her, he turned into some kind of alpha-male.

Cocky. Arrogant. He'd no idea where it came from. He was a straight up kind of guy, taught by his mom to treat women with respect. No wonder Cat kept turning him down. It was clear he needed to alter his approach.

Throwing the final item into his toolkit, he snorted. "No! Maybe I should finally get the message and let it go."

"What message?"

The sultry timbre of her voice made anything sound inviting. Like a bee to nectar, Mason honed in on the lure to find Cat standing in the open doorway. She wore a sexy little nothing of a summer dress, looking sweet as sunshine and hot as hellfire. His mouth watered and his dick jerked and he was right back wallowing in it big time.

"Umm," he muttered. "Nothing…nothing at all."

"Talk to yourself often?" She swayed forward, her laughter a light tease to his senses and his ego.

Mason chose diversion, pointing at the tub in the room, now his own personal elephant-in-the-room because he'd never be able to see it without imagining her in it. "It's all done, and your studio and B&B are good to go. After the inspector's visit on Monday, you'll be ready for business."

Pleasure lit her face, warming Mason again, but higher up this time, in the lonely place that was usually empty and cold.

"It's gorgeous. And ginormous. Thank you so much." She circled the tub admiring it while he admired her. "You're a miracle worker too, cause I saw the invoice you emailed and it's a third less than the original tub. How'd you manage it?"

Her praise and adoring smile shot Mason from warm to scorching hot.

Shit! Not again.

He yanked the toolkit from the table to cover his crotch. "We lucked out. I've a friend in the homebuilding biz, and this beauty got rejected before it could be installed because of a slight flaw. There's a small scratch on the other side, but I was able to buff it out, mostly. Hope that's okay?"

Cat walked around it again. "Hardly shows at all. Thank you for saving me so much money."

Mason watched as she twirled around, her face glowing as she took in the nearly empty studio. He looked forward to seeing her at work in here, creating her masterpieces. If she'd let him.

"I can't believe it," she murmured, once again beaming his way. "Only one more thing left to do in here and I can—"

"Did I forget something?"

That stopped Cat up short and her eyes darted away. "No, um. I just meant, you know, move in some supplies and tables."

"I'd be happy to help." He stepped closer, hoping for a chance to spend more time with her.

Her pretty blue eyes flitted back to his, startled and… alarmed. Odd.

Then she smiled, but it seemed forced. "You've done so much already. And it's practically nothing. Really."

"I don't mind at all."

"Well, actually, I've got four friends coming up from L.A. in a couple weeks and they're planning to help, but thanks anyway."

Mason nodded. "Sure. Okay." He silently questioned why "practically nothing" required four friends. And he wondered if one of those "friends" was really a special someone. His gut twisted, but it was none of his business.

"I really can't thank you enough, and I want you to know that I will Yelp you a great one. Tell everyone how pleased I am with the remodel."

"Thanks. I can always use more good reviews." He looked about but there was nothing more to do. "So, I guess I'll be going then."

"Sure. Yeah. I really do appreciate all you've done. Um." It seemed like Cat was stalling too. "It's super hot out and you've worked hard all week and it's Friday. Can I offer you a glass of lemonade?"

"No, but if you've got a cold beer," he joked, knowing she considered herself a wine connoisseur.

"I do have beer in the fridge. Locally brewed too."

Mason felt the world shift in his favor, not much, but an opening. "I'd love it. Thanks."

He left his toolkit by the truck and followed her up the lane, her new dogs trotting along behind them.

It felt good.

Within minutes Mason was gently rocking on the wooden swing of the large verandah that crossed the front of the farmhouse and curved around the side. He had a cold one in his hand and a hot Cat perched at his side.

It felt great.

Mason took a long draft from the bottle and then looked at the label. "This is good. Local you say?"

"I want to serve only local products, whenever possible. Thanks again for recommending Main Street Grocers. The owner's been a fount of information on local wineries and brewers. Plus, he carries most local brands right there, saving me from running all over the place, trying everything out."

"No problem." His voice sounded stubbly and gruff, emotion clogging his throat. "How do you like St. Helena so far?"

"I love it! Of course, I've always loved it here. When I was a kid I spent almost every July here with my aunt and uncle. They never had kids of their own, and I guess I was sort of loaned out as a temp child, but I adored them and they doted on me."

"So we might have met back then, although I admit I don't remember you."

Cat laughed. "I would have been a hair-in-a-ponytail rug-rat to your high school Adonis-ness. There's no freaking way you would have noticed me."

Mason wasn't so sure. Not that he would have lusted after a child, of course, but he just couldn't imagine not being fascinated on some level by Cat's spunk and cuteness. "I think the more likely answer is that I was busy working in my dad's business every summer, and by the time you were in high school I was gone in the army."

"Sometimes my whole family would gather here for different holidays, but my favorite visit was once in springtime. My aunt loved tulips…they're my favorite too…and this place comes alive with the pretty flowers every spring. Even now, they're everywhere, hiding under the ground waiting." She looked about expectantly, and Mason could almost see the fields of flowers too.

"So that's why you named it Tulip House."

"Yes. I was completely blown away when I learned that my aunt had left me the place a couple years ago. I'd just started a prestigious job managing the Malibu Inn. It's a ritzy little boutique hotel near the coast for friends and family of

Hollywood stars and the like. I wasn't ready to quit and move to the middle of nowhere."

"We're not exactly Timbuktu," he countered.

"No, um." Cat shrugged. "I do love St. Helena, but there isn't exactly a…club scene here, and I wasn't sure how I could make a living. But then I came up with the idea of making this wonderful place into a B&B and using the wine house for…"

"…an art studio," he finished when she didn't.

After a second's hesitation, Cat nodded.

Mason wanted to learn more about her art, but seeing the dogs frolicking in the grass, he asked, "Why'd you name the bigger dog Peanut? Looks more like a horse than a dog."

"Didn't name them, actually. They came that way."

When their play tumbled into her rose garden, Cat leaned forward, yelling, "Peanut and Gringo, come!" They immediately raced over for some lovin' and Mason watched as she scratched each one under their chins. Their thumping tails and worshipful eyes a sign that they were in doggie heaven. He would be too, if she fondled him like that…*anywhere.*

Mason reached over to pat Peanut on the head. They were both friendly and amazingly protective of a woman they'd barely known a week. "He's just massive. Half Great Dane, I'd say, and his black and white coloring makes me think the other half's Dalmatian."

"Yeah, but it's only a guess. Their former owner wanted protection after her husband died and got them as puppies from a shelter. There's no paper trail beyond that. The smaller one's obviously a German Shepard mix." She leaned off the swing to hug Gringo, arms wrapped around him and burying her face in the dog's freshly groomed hair.

Mason wished he were a dog.

Geez! Was there anything Cat could do that wouldn't heat his blood? He tipped the bottle and downed the rest of his beer. "So you don't know why they've such odd names?"

"Yeah I do." She chuckled again. "The elderly lady called them Pinot and Grigio after her favorite wine, and over time the names morphed."

Mason chortled. "What is it about everyone around here. They're all nutso about wine, if you ask me."

"Of course they are. On some level, it's everyone's business here in Napa Valley. Soon it'll be mine too." She made a swiping motion, as if wiping everything away. "No vineyards, no reason for a B&B. I mean it's pretty 'n all up here, but…"

"I get it and, honestly, I don't think Steele Plumbing would be doing so well if it weren't for all the building and refurb work the weekenders bring." He raised his empty bottle in salute. "However, here's to more new breweries like this one. Beagle Dog Brewery, huh. It's good. I like the malty taste, sort of like molasses."

"So now you sound nutso about beer," she teased.

He pretended indignation. "There's no such thing as too much beer-love. Greatest drink on earth."

"Right." And they both laughed.

She raised her merlot, the late sun's rays catching the dark hue and turning it a rich, thick scarlet, and clinked her glass against his bottle. "So I guess you'll think I'm nutso too, cause I named my wine house the Burgundy Rose."

"That's a pretty name. Do most artists name their studios?"

Cat's easy smile drained away, and she tipped her wineglass and drained it next. "Don't know. Probably."

Mason wondered what he'd said. "I can't wait to see some of your work. I saw the tulip paintings you recently hung inside the house. Did you do those?"

"No. Picked them up cheap at a discount store."

"Why not decorate with some of your own art. I'm sure it would make the whole place more unique. Is it all still down in L.A.?"

Now Cat looked distinctly uncomfortable, so he added, "I'm sure I'll love it, if that's your concern? I'm just interested to see what inspires you."

"Yeah, well, someday, maybe." She jumped up from the wooden swing. "You're empty. I'll get you another." And bolted inside.

Shit! What did I say?

Maybe Cat was one of those artists that never showed their work, who left barns full of masterpieces to be discovered after they were dead. Mason ran a frustrated hand through his hair. It'd been going so well.

He followed her inside to see if everything was okay and found Cat crossing off another date on her big project calendar. She looked up when he came bursting through the screen door. Capping her big red marker, she said "Another day, another step closer to opening. And only a little behind schedule. Thank you again for doing the work so quickly."

"They don't call me racin' Mason for nothing. But you get half the credit. You've put in a ton of sweat equity yourself."

"Here you go." She handed him another cold one from the fridge and refilled her glass.

"Thanks."

He followed her out to the porch, preoccupied with trying to guess what he'd said to upset her. "About the art, I hope I didn't offend—"

"Tell me about yourself?" Cat interrupted his thoughts. "I already know you took over your dad's business a couple years ago, but what did you do before that? Is your dad retired? Does he still live in the area? And what do you like to do on your time off?"

Clearly, she wanted to keep him too busy talking about himself to remember she hadn't answered *any* of his questions. He'd follow her lead if it would bring a smile back to her face. Mason had cataloged all of her expressions—sweet, teasing, humorous—and liked them all. His favorite was the dreamy one Cat sometimes wore when she gazed around the inside of her future art studio. He'd like it very much if he were the one to make her look so sexy.

"Okay then," he said. "Army sergeant. Yes. No. Not much." He took a swig of his beer and smirked at her. "What about you, *Fernball?*" He drawled it out, liking the way her eyes fired at his teasing.

"Oh come on!" She punched him in the upper arm, hard, but he didn't care. The spot where she'd touched his skin tingled and lit a small spark down below. If she ever actually caressed him with intent, he'd combust.

"Well?" she urged.

Mason cleared his throat. "Not that much to tell, really. I was born and raised here in St. Helena and did two stints in Iraq after high school."

"I bet you were captain of the football team."

"Nope. I did track and field, which didn't impress the girls as much. Though I did captain that team."

"Hmm…I can imagine you making running shorts and a tank top look pretty damn hot."

Mason laughed, pleased that she was flirting. He wanted to seize the chance to ask her out again, but stopped himself.

Enjoy the moment. Don't press her.

"Was it hard? Iraq, I mean?"

"Yeah. I made some lifelong buddies in the military, and then lost some friends too. But that's not why I didn't reenlist. My dad needed to move to a dryer climate. He's in Arizona with my mom now, and we'd always planned that I'd take over. I worked at Steele Plumbing all through my teens. So when my second term was up, I came home."

"I bet your high school sweetheart was happy to have you back." She'd said it lightly, but he heard the question there.

"No, actually, they'd all married or moved away by then."

"They?" She tilted her head, her eyes twinkling. "So track and field worked for you after all."

He grinned broadly. No reason to deny it.

Cat looked down at her hand and seemed to be counting off on her fingers. "So that just leaves…what do you like to do when you're not working?"

Not much!

He'd told her that already, but not why. And now it was Mason's turn to feel uncomfortable. He contemplated his beer bottle, trying to decide how much to reveal. Could he tell her that at first, when he'd arrived home from Iraq, he'd just wanted to get his bearings after those horrific years. That he'd thrown himself into building his business as a way to avoid dumping his emotional baggage on anyone, even his family. That eventually all he knew was work and work…and more work. And, lastly, that when he finally felt grounded and ready for a life without an M-4 carbine rifle in his arms and a pack on his back, there was no one left waiting for him. No one to love.

And now there was.

And her name was Cat.

And she soothed and refreshed him like a summer shower on a hot day.

But he realized, finally, he'd played it all wrong with her. Jumped right back into his youthful braggadocio, which had served him just fine with teenage girls all those years ago but didn't work with a mature woman.

Mason glanced at her, and saw that she was perfectly happy to give him all the time he needed. There was a calmness or perhaps passivity to her manner, suggesting she had practice with waiting and remaining silent.

The urge to pull Cat in his arms, to bury himself in her, was overwhelming. A physical demand that made him jump to his feet before he acted on it.

"I've got to go," he said, loping down the porch steps. "Thanks for the brew." He waved and started toward his truck parked back by the wine house.

"Um. Okay then. Bye," she called, bewilderment sounding in the way she trailed it out.

Mason paused, drew a deep breath, and faced her from halfway down the lane. "I pretty much work all the time. As for what I like to do when I'm not working?" he repeated her question.

"I like to spend time with you."

Cat stood then, and he felt her eyes on him as he climbed into his truck. He'd probably blown it big time. A hermit basket-case didn't have a chance with a beautiful, confident woman like her.

Gunning the motor, Mason waved once as he raced by Cat where she stood at the verandah's railing. She didn't return the gesture.

Chapter 3

~ I like to spend time with you

Cat was on edge. She'd changed her clothes three times as the afternoon dragged. First a sexy nothing of a dress, then a businesslike blouse and skirt, and now casual shorts and t-shirt paired with strappy, heeled sandals.

I like to spend time with you.

Mason's revelation had replayed over and over in her mind all weekend. Just seven simple words that didn't feel simple at all.

Cat prowled the front parlor waiting for three o'clock when Mason and the town inspector would arrive. She felt unsettled. Mason's surprising declaration had stirred her like a primitive mating call, making her as hot and bothered as a wild animal in heat. But she couldn't get past the idea that their sexual practices would be incompatible—like two different species trying to get it on.

She should be focused on the all-important inspection, but all Cat could think about was Mason. It's not like he'd pledged his undying love. Hadn't even tried to ask her out again. And he hadn't called once in the three days since he'd told her how he felt.

I like to spend time with you.

"Get a grip," Cat mumbled. She needed to get her head on straight but was majorly conflicted. She wanted Mason to want her even though she felt certain they would not work as a couple.

The sound of an approaching truck made her heart jump in her chest, and through the window she saw that it was Mason. She glanced at the mantel clock and read two-thirty. He'd come early.

I like to spend time with you.

Maybe she'd surprise him and ask him out, and that thought made her feel springy and light as she followed his truck to the Burgundy Rose.

And then Mason was out of his truck, standing before her. He paused good and long, taking her in, and her sub training allowed her to stand tall and proud before him for as long as he wanted to look. Her training had also taught her something else—how to present her assets to best sexy effect. Her short shorts and tall wedge sandals showed off her long lean legs, and her breezy low-cut blouse offered glimpses of cleavage. A push-up bra helped too.

Mason let fly a deep wolf-whistle.

"New hair?" he asked with a wink, and Cat knew that he was back in full form. Both versions of the man lit her up— cocky or intense—but she wished for a little more time with the other Mason, the darkly sincere one who'd pledged something she found impossible to resist.

"Ha ha," she rejoined, keeping it light, before turning away to open the door.

He doesn't know the real me, she reminded herself. But for the first time in many years, Cat wished that she were different, that her needs were more mundane. Normal. That a great guy like Mason would be enough for her. And she wondered if maybe she should try normal out again, that with him it might be different this time.

"Welcome to the Burgundy Rose." She plastered a peppy, lighthearted expression on her face and gestured for him to enter.

* * *

Following her lead, Mason walked through the door.

He was at a loss. He'd managed the cocky wolf-whistle because speech was impossible at the moment.

God you look good! It was about the only thought in his head.

He ate her up, his eyes traveling the length of her body. It was a view he would never get tired of, whether fully dressed, naked in his fantasies, or, like now, revealing lots of skin but not enough.

When he didn't speak, Cat filled the gap. "I've finished hanging the curtains and every room in the farmhouse is clean and ready to go." He barely heard her. "I'm thrilled that everything's done. And, I've got bookings through the New Year."

"That's nice," he mumbled. Still staring, head tilted, he fixated on her pert breasts.

"I tried it out last night." Cat pointed at the claw-foot tub.

That got his attention. Mason's eyes shot to the empty tub sitting in the middle of the room.

But it wasn't empty. Not in his mind.

Cat was there, lying in the tub, soaking in the warm water. Naked. Bubbles barely covering her. The whole fantasy as real to him as if he could touch it. Touch her. *Shit!* He would touch her all right, hands lathered with soap, sliding from behind to wash, then caress her breasts. His lips on the soft skin at the curve of her neck. Hands slipping into the water all the way down to the swollen flesh between her—"

"Earth to Mason." She tapped on his shoulder.

"Wha…"

He heard laughter, twinkling, happy, and bright.

Mason had to blink several times until he found himself back in a near empty room facing a completely empty tub.

"Where'd you go, Mason? You were like a thousand miles away."

He sensed she knew exactly where he'd been. A swift glance over his shoulder at Cat's amused expression told him he was right, but he didn't care. She was surprisingly close. Mason pivoted, and she was within kissing distance. He stared at her pretty pink mouth and leaned in. She remained still, didn't pull back. Mason moved closer, his hands reaching for her…

He hesitated, unsure why.

Felt an odd rumbling. A train? It seemed to come from afar but be all around him at the same time.

Then it started in full. Terror. He could hear it, see it, feel it. Like a slow-motion locomotive plowing through the valley of hell.

Mason knew the instant Cat realized what was happening. Her eyes grew huge and haunted. She screamed. He swept her up into his arms to start for the open door, fighting for footing against the violent shaking beneath him. Barely making progress, he worried the creaking, torqueing beams would tumble the roof down upon them.

Mason held her tightly, but she held him tighter, burying her face in his chest as if he were her salvation. But still, she screamed.

And then, like that, it was over.

The ground settled. The rumbling vanished. But Cat continued to cry out, pulling at him as if only he could save her from the abyss.

"Shhh," he soothed. "It's okay." Mason carried her out into the bright sunshine. "Shhh." He hugged her and showered kisses across her forehead and in her hair, nuzzling her.

Cat continued to shake and sob and grasp at him like her existence depended on it.

"It's over now. *Shhh*. It's okay. We're alright."

She was hysterical and, not knowing what to do, Mason went alpha male on her. In a firm, authoritative voice, he commanded, "Cat! Stop this. You need to listen to me and calm down."

Surprising him, she immediately settled, her sobs turning to whimpers. Her death grip loosening.

Mason couldn't figure out what was happening with her. He had been through worse earthquakes. He'd be surprised if there was any real damage from this one.

"Shhh," he soothed, but quickly changed tactics, going alpha male again, because that had seemed to work. "You. Are. Okay! You need to hear me, Cat."

She nodded against his chest. Slowly she lifted her tear-streaked face and their eyes met. She sucked in a harsh breath, her eyes huge.

"Mason?" It was as if she were confused it was him there with her and not someone else. Then Cat seemed to realize she was in his arms and outside. She took a longer, deeper breath. "I'm okay now. Could you please release me."

Gently, Mason eased her to the ground, wondering once again at her strange phrasing. He kept her close at his side, supporting her. "Are you sure? Let's sit down."

He walked Cat to the wrought-iron bench near a small rose garden. Burgundy colored blooms, of course. He smiled. *Yeah*, she had an artist's eye, even if, apparently no completed art.

They sat, and Mason kept his arm around her shoulders. "Tell me about it?"

She sniffled and wiped her eyes. Looking down at her lap, she whispered, "It's stupid, really. When I was about four years old, I was in a big earthquake. Loma Prieta. We'd been up to visit auntie and we were all in San Francisco for a day of sightseeing." Cat shuddered as if the memory was too awful to contemplate.

"And?" Mason urged, needing to understand so he could help her.

"When it hit, I was near a window and it shattered. I don't remember much but the chaos and the screaming. I was so afraid, even with my mother right there. I was cut bad and ended up in the E.R. And in the hospital there was moaning and so much blood and pain. Mostly mine."

Cat pulled away from him then and turned to show him her back. Lifting the hem of her blouse, she revealed a long scar. Without thought, Mason reached out and drew his finger down the faint ridge that ran down half her back. She didn't pull away.

"My injury was nothing, really. Lots of people died. Sixty-three in total. I just got stitches and it wasn't life threatening. So you see, I'm just being silly to carry—"

"No!"

It came out more strident than he'd intended, but Mason needed her to hear him. "You went through a traumatic experience at a very young age. The gory things you witnessed. Anyone would be affected by it, and you have a right to your feelings." He eased her back against him and gently patted her shoulder. "But, today, you are fine. Not hurt. I can't see any outward damage to the wine house either."

Cat nodded resolutely and pushed away to sit upright. "I'm okay." It made his chest tight to see her bravery.

"Hello," yelled a man's voice. "Everyone okay?"

They looked up to see the inspector, Bart Peterson, coming around the corner of the wine house.

"We're fine," Mason called. "Just a little shaken up."

"Good, but you need to hurry. Something's wrong at the house. Water blasting everywhere."

Dread landed like a heavy brick in Mason's gut. He lurched off the bench to chase after an already sprinting Cat. Rounding the corner of the wine house it was a relief to spy the grand old Victorian farmhouse intact, standing proud and elegant. No collapsed verandah or shattered windows. The carved moldings on the eaves still attached.

They both reached it at the same time and saw the problem. A fountain of water spewing up right in the center of the rose garden at the front of the house. The old pipes had sprung a leak when the ground shifted. A pond was already forming where the runoff collected in the yard.

"I'll cut the water," Mason yelled jogging toward the pump house around back. From the corner of his eye, he saw Cat run up the steps into the house. The shaker was only about a 4 or 5 pointer, he guessed. The structure should be sound. He hoped.

Within minutes they met back at the porch, the inspector there waiting for them, reading his smartphone. With the water cut, the little pond was already slipping away into the earth. Cat looked agitated but thankfully not panicked.

"The inside looks fine," she reported. "A couple glasses broke in my cupboard but that's all. Even the basement's dry, thank heavens!" Surprisingly, her face blossomed into a huge smile. "I made it! My first big quake and I'm okay. Everything's okay."

"It's a good thing you were here to cut the water before any of it could flow back into the house," Peterson told them.

"Yeah."

But Mason didn't feel good about it. He ran a hand through his hair and paced the porch. He could see the ramifications but he guessed Cat hadn't yet. "I spot checked all the pipes. Your aunt remodeled the kitchen and created the master suite just eight years ago, and at that time it was fully checked by my dad, but I guess some of the larger pipes in the yard are weak. I should've caught it." He turned to Cat, "I'm sorry."

"No, Mason," Peterson interrupted. "Short of digging up the entire property, there's no way you could have checked every inch of pipe, and reports are this was a surface quake." He glanced down at his phone to read the latest update. "I'm sure there are ruptured pipes and buckled roadways all through the area."

Cat still didn't look overly worried. She walked right up to him and took hold of his hand, squeezing it. "It's not your fault. Mr. Peterson's right. You've done an amazing job here and I'll always be grateful." Their eyes held, and Mason wanted very much to gather her back into his arms.

"I'll be going then," said Peterson. "Just call to reschedule once the repairs are done."

"Wait, what?" Cat pulled away from Mason to look at the inspector. "Can't you do it anyway?" It only took a moment for her to realize the futility of her request. "Could you at least check the wine house? It wasn't affected."

"Sure," he said. "I guess I can do that."

While Peterson checked the wine house, Mason and she discussed the repairs. He promised to get started evaluating and repairing it right away. If the damage wasn't system wide, Mason guessed he could finish repairs in less than a week, but Cat got more bad news from the inspector when she tried to reschedule the inspection.

"I'm sorry Miss Morrison. I'm leaving town for a family wedding tomorrow. When I get back I'm booked solid for two weeks, and that was before the earthquake. We have a part-time inspector too, but even if he jumps to full-time, it could be a month or more."

"No!" she cried. "That won't work. I've got guests coming before then."

"I'm sorry, but this quake's going to hurt lots of folks around here, I'm sure." He smiled kindly, before heading down the porch steps. "Mason, email me when the repairs are done."

"But…" Cat's face crumpled. Mason could see she was fighting for control, her eyes taking on that panicked, haunted look again. He stepped toward her, ready to gather her into his arms if she'd let him.

"I've gotta check something," Cat called, hurrying into the house. Mason followed her to the kitchen. She went straight to her big project calendar and started counting off days, counting lost bookings, and seeming to do mental calculations in her head. When she faced him again, the panic had morphed into something worse. Despair etched her face and showed in the slump of her shoulders. She looked defeated.

"It's not that bad," he soothed. "I'll get the repairs done ASAP. So you lost a couple weeks of revenue, maybe a month. You'll be all right."

"You don't understand." She collapsed into a kitchen chair, her head in her hands. "It's over. I've lost."

Mason didn't know what to do. He poured her a glass of water and placed it on the table in front of her, then sat across from her. "Tell me what's going on. We can figure this out together."

She raised her head slowly and lifted her eyes to him. He saw a glimmer of hope. "Thank you for promising to get the work done quickly."

He leaned across the table and squeezed her hands. "I'll work double-time."

"So, maybe, if you get it done quickly, maybe the inspector can squeeze me in, and I can still open on time."

Mason glanced away, focusing on the fridge calendar. He didn't want to watch her hope drain away. "I'm sorry, Cat. I really am. But my guess is that the work will take at least a week, even if I work nights. I'll try to push off my other jobs, but…then there's still the inspection. It just doesn't look likely we'll get it done in time. I know you're on a tight budget, but why's it such a problem?"

She didn't answer. Just kept staring at her hands.

"If you're worried about making your loan payment, we can go to the bank together. Reassure them that your business plan is solid and show them that you've got bookings lined up. I know it looks bleak, but—"

"I don't have any bank loans." Her eyes had that haunted look again. "They all turned me down. Even with the equity in the house, it wasn't enough to get a ninety thousand dollar bank loan to cover the remodeling."

"That doesn't make sense. This estate is worth—"

"I had bad credit. In the past, I messed up, big time. I've worked hard to overcome it, but no legitimate bank would lend me the money."

Mason straightened, worry rattling through him. "Please tell me you didn't use a loan shark?"

"No, not exactly."

That didn't reassure him. He waited but she didn't say more. "Please tell me. Maybe I can think of something. You know, two heads are better than one."

Cat studied him, taking several deep breaths. She appeared to be judging whether she could trust him, and he tried to look calmer than he felt, open and worthy of her secrets.

Finally she nodded. "My old friends lent me some money, and my aunt left some funds, explicitly to cover property taxes. I had a small savings too, not much but some. Together, that only covered twenty percent of what I needed." She hesitated again.

Mason grasped her hands and this time didn't let go. "You can trust me."

She took another deep breath and nodded. "The biggest part came from a guy down in Malibu...a sort of former boyfriend, I guess you could call him. He's super rich and seventy-thousand dollars means nothing to him."

Mason let out the breath he'd been holding in a big whoosh, along with the fear that was choking him. "That's great then. I'm sure he'll understand. It's a freak'n earthquake after all, nothing you did wrong."

"It's not that simple. He didn't want to let me go. The loan was his way of keeping me connected to him. He hopes I'll fail because there are several triggers written into the agreement that will keep me tied to him."

"I don't understand."

"The first payment is due November 1st. If I fail to meet it... Now, it's *when* I fail, he gets to take over the business."

Mason reared back. He jumped up and turned away from Cat, pretending to need a glass of water himself. He wanted to drill into her, demand to know how she could do something so incredibly stupid.

"I'm not totally crazy, Mason," she said to his back. "Just desperate, at the time, to get away from..."

He looked back at her sharply.

"I mean desperate to make the B&B a reality. And I have a great deal of experience in the hospitality business. I've told you about how I worked in my parent's inn growing up in Palm Desert. After I moved to L.A., I had various hotel jobs, working my way up to manager, but my real break came when I landed the Malibu Inn. Lynch helped me get it."

Mason had a name now and he seized on it.

Lynch.

His stomach churned at the idea that Cat's ex still controlled her. Jealousy filled him. That this former lover had played such an important role in her life, helped her in ways he never could. That Lynch was still instrumental to her future, while he was nothing to her but a contractor.

Mason barely heard the rest. That she'd padded the business plan, built in extra time and extra funds. He now knew why the big calendar held such importance to her, like a hallowed ritual the way she carefully crossed off every day and every goal met.

"Look, will it help if you defer the last payment on my contract. I bet even Walt will understand if the tub is paid late. It was just sitting there unwanted in his store anyway. Or, maybe, I could make you a bridge loan. I've seen the tremendous effort you've put in here. I know the B&B is going to be a huge success once you get going."

Cat shook her head as she stood up. She walked past him to the sink, chin high, shoulders back. "No thank you. It's my mess and I'm an adult. I'll figure it out. It's not like I'll lose the place or even the income from it. It's just that I'll have to let someone else manage it and become…never mind. It doesn't matter."

Mason sensed that whatever Cat hadn't said did matter, a heck of a lot.

But it was obvious she was done talking. He looked at his watch and told her he'd get started on the work right away since it was only four. He'd have said anything if it would wipe that bleak look off her face. Then Cat thanked him again, saying she'd better sweep up the broken glass and check that there wasn't any damage in the wine house. Later on, she made him a sandwich for dinner, which Mason ate standing up with a glass of lemonade. He wanted to keep working.

When darkness started to fall, he considered going back to the shop and grabbing some portable work lights to keep going, but he had administrivia that would keep him up late into the night. At the very least, he needed to reach out to his two contract employees for more assistance and check email to see if any of his other clients had plumbing issues because of the earthquake. He'd ignored his cell all afternoon, leaving it turned off, but now it was time he faced his obligations.

Cat came out as he was packing his truck. She seemed, if not happy, like she had regained some of her pluck. She was the kind of hard-working woman that wouldn't stay down for long, and that eased his tight chest.

Standing by the open door of his pickup, he said, "I'll be back as soon as possible to keep at it. I'm really sorry this happened."

"It's not your fault." She meant it too. Even in the fading light, he could see gratitude in her expression, her eyes sunny, and then, surprisingly, she beamed a smile at him that could light his very soul. "You've become an incredible friend, and that means a lot to me."

"Still, I wish there was something more I could do."

Her grin broadened, and she winked. "You could ask me out again." He was certain she meant it as a joke.

But Mason didn't care, he'd take any opening she gave him. His offer came out more like a gruff order than an invitation. "Go out with me, Cat."

"My, my. So commanding," she teased. "But okay."

Her willing compliance did something to Mason, and he went a little Neanderthal. "Friday night. Wear something pretty and dressy."

Her eyes rounded at his authoritarian manner, but before he could lessen it, Cat quietly replied, "Yes, sir."

Something primal stirred in Mason at her obedient purr and the way she shyly dropped her gaze downward. Cat had transformed into a sex kitten. Soft, feminine, willing. He didn't understand it, had never felt this way before, but her sweet manner—whatever it was that she was doing—ignited unfamiliar needs in him. Overwhelming alpha-male, take-control needs. A primitive, deep-in-the-amygdala rush to claim her, mate her in an aggressive way he'd never done before and couldn't quite comprehend.

If she acted like this in the bedroom, he was a goner.

Sucking a harsh breath, Mason realized he had to leave—*now*—before he acted on this new type of lust. However, instinct wouldn't let the moment pass without another foray into this new world.

"Be ready at seven o'clock sharp." He climbed into his truck and looked at her through the open window. Hand on the ignition he waited for it.

"Yes, sir," she called melodiously.

He grinned and gunned the engine.

Laughing in delight, Mason waved at Cat, who stood watching as he drove away. This new thing was weird but awesome. He may not get what had just happened, but he'd pursue it with one hundred percent enthusiasm just to see that sexy, dreamy look on Cat's face one more time.

Chapter 4

~ Peanut and Gringo

The next morning, hot coffee in hand, Cat stared uselessly at the project calendar. She wished it would morph before her eyes, stretch, grow extra days, warp the space time continuum, *whatever*. Just so long as she had the leeway to catch up before it was time to pay the piper, because her piper didn't play a flute, and the reed he used would land squarely on her backside.

Cat shrugged and turned away. She hadn't gotten this far in life by giving up, and she wouldn't start now.

Gathering up the garbage, which was mostly broken glass, she carried it out the kitchen door. The earthquake had done more damage to her glassware and bottles in her pantry than she'd originally realized.

"Peanut! Gringo!" she called, and within seconds they came loping around the side of the farmhouse from the little outdoor homes where they slept, always on the job guard-dogging her place. The three of them walked down the driveway to drop the garbage at the curb. Seeing the Meadowood Vintner sign down the road, Cat remembered that this was one wine she hadn't yet tried, and since they were neighbors she really should talk to them about cross promotion. However, if she didn't retain control of the property it would all be a big waste of time.

Cat had just made it back to the porch when she heard the phone ringing. Running up the steps two at a time, she rushed inside and let the screen door swing shut, leaving the dogs peering inside, tails wagging.

"Hello," she chirped, making it way more cheery than she felt. "Tulip House Bed and Breakfast."

"Pussycat. How are you?" The magnificently deep, commanding timbre was tinged with concern, but her Dom's voice no longer made her swoon. "When you didn't return my calls yesterday I nearly hopped on a plane to see you." Now she heard censure.

"I'm sorry, Sir. I was just so busy cleaning up the mess." Cat crossed her fingers at the tiny fabrication. "But I'm fine, Sir."

"No part of you is damaged?"

"No, Sir. Not a scratch." Lynch considered it his sole right to mark her, mar her beauty. In his world, no one, not even mother earth, should dare cross him.

"Is there anything else?" he asked.

She hesitated. She should tell him about the burst pipe and all that it meant, but Cat couldn't bring herself to shorten the time she had left before surrendering to him. And maybe there was still a way out she hadn't thought of yet.

"Bastet." The quality was flat, but his use of the detested slave name told her he was exasperated. Then she realized why.

He knows!

She didn't know how, but Cat was absolutely certain Lynch already knew about the burst pipe. It stunned her, still to this day, that his deep voice could convey so much meaning in one word. Reproach. Displeasure. Retribution.

She opened her mouth to admit the B&B delay but nothing came out. Standing frozen, phone to ear, she was physically unable to utter the words that would end her dreams.

At one time, she'd been in awe of him, perhaps even in love. He was all-powerful in his Hollywood circles. Handsome. Generous. Superbly satisfying as a lover, when he felt his playmates warranted it. He'd been her advocate, protector, teacher. Now he wanted to raise her above everyone else in their circle to become the *favored* of his crazy harem. Or the lowest of the low, depending on his mood.

When he had first added her to his stable, Lynch had dubbed her Pussycat—or just Pussy—having rejected Cat as too bland for his harem and Catriona too regal for a sub. The day he'd made his intentions known that he would favor her, Lynch had added another moniker, because every house slave wore a sex goddess name, literally, on a collar around their neck. Hers would be Bastet, the feline Egyptian goddess of sexuality and domesticity. He thought it perfect, expecting docile servitude in his home and wild sexuality in his playroom. Even though she wasn't officially one of his house slaves yet, this was the name he now used when he was unhappy with her. She hated it.

"Bastet!" He was becoming angry.

Shivers ricocheted down her stiff spine and chilled Cat. Her mind locked up, not delicious subspace but icy limbo. It was the mental place she went to whenever his "attentions" became too extreme. Soon this would be her permanent state. She would cease to be flowing and free, becoming instead an ice princess locked away in a frozen dungeon. It would be swanky and glamorous, but a prison nonetheless.

"Sir. There is some—" Her whisper trembled.

"Speak up. I can't hear you."

"Yes, Sir," Cat responded reflexively, but still too quietly. She cleared her throat and began again. "A main pipe outside burst and that meant the inspector couldn't—"

"Yes, yes, I know all this, but consider yourself warned. Next time don't attempt to keep anything from me."

"Yes, Sir." She'd broken a rule and been given a free pass. "Thank you, Sir."

The dogs outside whimpered, sensing her distress. Putting her hand over the phone, she soothed quietly, "It's okay, boys."

"I am truly sorry this happened," Lynch said. "I know how you cherish your aunt's home, and I don't want you to worry about it. *Together,* we'll get it fixed up in no time. And, in a way this is good news."

"Good news?"

"I am fully cognizant that this is an enormous step, finally accepting your place by my side. It's not an easy choice, I know, and that makes your gift mean so much more." He sounded almost excited, but her Dom didn't get excited. Not over his girls anyway. "I've understood all along that you didn't really want to leave me. Needing a little push, as it were, to give up your freedom is totally understandable given the magnitude of your new position."

The burgeoning glee in his voice shocked her, so unlike Master to show any emotion. It told Cat that he wanted this way more than she had realized and that he considered it a done deal. The thought of her gilded prison waiting in Malibu turned her as cold as if she really were locked in ice. She needed more time.

"Sir, I still have seven weeks before the first payment."

"You know full well you're not going to make it, so why wait? It's what you agreed to when you signed your name on those two contracts. I want you down here with me. Where you belong."

Panic clutched at Cat, her chest so tight, she couldn't breathe.

"What if I refuse?"

"Don't push me." She could hear his rising ire. "Do that and I'll take full control of the B&B and bar you from ever setting foot on the grounds again."

"It's my place! You can't do that," she cried. "And, anyway, no court is going to enforce a slave contract. I'm sure it's not legal."

He made a familiar tsking sound. She cringed, knowing what it usually signified. At least, for the moment, four hundred miles separated his crop from her ass.

"I thought it meant something to you when you signed our pact," he chided. "It certainly meant a great deal to me. It distresses me that you could turn your back on it. On me." He didn't sound upset, more like irate.

"Regardless," he continued all business now, "the loan agreement is completely legal, my lawyers made sure of that, and it states that if the payments aren't made on schedule, the business becomes a partnership with me in charge. But you know this all already. Still, it's complicated, so I'll try to help you understand. I structured this for your benefit, as a way to protect your inheritance, so that no matter how much you messed up, I'll be there to ensure the business is a success."

For my benefit, my ass. Cat gritted her teeth. "Okay, but nothing in that agreement can force me to become your live-in house slave."

"Bastet!" Lynch had yelled into the phone. "You agreed to it. Willingly signed both documents before witnesses. So listen to what I'm about to say, because while I can't legally enforce your slave contract, I can and will implement the terms of the loan agreement and take over the B&B. That means, that if you don't get your ass down here and turn yourself over to my keeping, I'll run it into the ground. Bankrupt the business. You'll lose your aunt's place in foreclosure."

"No! Please, Master. I'm begging you." Lynch was ruthless in his business dealings. Cat didn't doubt he would do it. She felt dizzy, nausea turning her stomach.

"Dearest, that's the last thing I want to do. But you need to honor your word. You know that as a Dom and a businessman, integrity and trust are qualities I value above all else. You're just confused by the stress of the earthquake, but once you're down here with me, I'll handle all your problems. The only thing you'll need to concern yourself with is being available for me. You know I have other subs for the heavy lifting." By that he meant, the heavy beatings. Chuckling, he added, "It'll be like a vacation."

He was full of shit. Cat had seen him in action too long, not to realize that. Oh, she acknowledged that he could "handle" her B&B all right, make it a huge success, but as for the carefree job of live-in sex slave. *Ha!* He'd make her life a living nightmare.

Lynch maintained a stable of three to four subs at all times—girls that had a degree of freedom and could go home when not in use—but the live-in was a full-time, 24/7, house slave. Available to serve whenever he needed in whatever capacity he desired. The slave had no other life. No day job. No apartment. No private space at all. And no voice, unless asked a question by him or one of his guests.

The live-in was both trophy and doormat. To broadcast his power and importance, Lynch often paraded his current beauty around at glamorous parties, dripping in jewels with eyes only for him. At other times, he ignored it, making her nothing more than living furniture. Naked, of course, unless they were outside his oceanfront estate.

Live-in's only lasted a year or two. Lynch needed the novelty of breaking in a new one. Cat had started searching for a way out the minute she'd learned he wanted her in this role. The shackles were tightening, but she wasn't ready to give up.

"Sir, I'll honor the slave contract when it's time, and I'm so grateful for all your help. It's just that I'd like to get the project as far along as possible before you hire a manager." She needed to tread carefully. "I'd like the full time that you granted in the agreement. That's all."

Silence greeted Cat. Would he try to force her?

It dragged on, and her gut tightened.

"My sweet Pussy, as long as we have an understanding, I'll allow the time stipulated in the loan agreement."

"I appreciate your patience. Thank you, Sir." The tightness loosened, and Cat silently sucked in air, trying to alleviate the dizziness. She had a reprieve, if not a pardon. It was something.

"And, anyway, I'll have a full weekend to eat my treat." He chuckled at his own pun.

"Sir?"

"When I come up for the dungeon building party. I plan to oversee the placement of the equipment from a Dom's perspective."

"Mistress Grace can do that. And you're so busy. Taking a whole weekend away from—"

"I insist. I'll see you in two weeks." Then he hung up.

Shit!

Cat looked at the phone in her hand. She couldn't stop him from coming, but at least the induction wouldn't happen here. Lynch always held a big party for the transition—the showman in him would never be happy with a private ceremony. He always wanted his Hollywood colleagues to witness the extreme power he wielded. Cat wished she'd never accepted the money, but then what? The project would never have broken ground.

Nervous energy made her pace around the kitchen. The dogs whimpered, their faces stuck to the screen. Cat opened the door. "Okay, you can come in, but just this one time."

She collapsed right down on the floor, exhaustion suddenly weighing her down. Peanut and Gringo rolled onto their backs, doggy eyes begging, and she reached over and scratched both their bellies at the same time.

"We'll be just fine, you'll see," she murmured. But was she trying to calm them or herself?

Chapter 5

~ *the Burgundy Rose dungeon*

Cat worked to distraction for the rest of the day. Cleaning the farmhouse to within an inch of its life. She drove down Highway 29 to the big discount store in Napa city to replace the broken glasses, then visited several local wineries, and anywhere else she could think of to keep her mind off the impending end to her aspirations.

But it was late now and the worry had settled back on her with the setting of the sun.

Puttering around her attic, she remembered that Lynch would expect her to wear his collar. Not the locked-in-place leather and steel version his house slave wore, but pretty style that decorated his harem. She rummaged around in the bottom drawer of her dresser where she'd stashed her kink-wear, hoping she hadn't misplaced it. That would make him irritated and suspicious.

"There you are." She pulled it out from under a leather corset and held it up to the light to admire the sparkling crystals. It really was very elegant. Each collar was unique, chosen specifically for each sub. Hers was a luxurious slate-gray leather studded with large, expensive Swarovski crystals, alternating pale pink and azure. The blue stones matched her eyes perfectly.

She'd been absolutely thrilled when Lynch had first put it around her neck, initiating her into his stable in a lavish party before hundreds at an exclusive private club. In the kink world, he was royalty and she'd been elevated to become one of his consorts.

For nearly three years she'd reveled in her role and all the lavish trappings, especially the amazing kinky sex. Cat had long since given up trying to understand her perverted desires. No childhood trauma had done this to her. No first fuck had fucked her up.

For years, she'd been secretly ashamed about her need for sexual domination, knowing that her parents, especially her feminist mom, would never understand. Lynch had helped her here too, helped Cat to let go of any lingering shame and fully accept herself—she was a submissive through and through, even if only for sex. In the bedroom or dungeon, she transformed into a compliant, subservient plaything, living only to serve others. It was who she was. It was the one thing that aroused Cat. *Always*. It was her own personal aphrodisiac.

Early on in their odd relationship, Lynch had trained her to his taste, and she'd worked tirelessly to improve her skills to please him. When he helped her secure the prestigious Malibu Inn position, she'd worked even harder, not wanting any failings on her part to reflect badly on him.

At first, she'd been in a constant state of euphoria—sexually and emotionally—but after a couple years she began to yearn for something more, a deeper emotional connection. She cared for Lynch, but theirs wasn't an equal love, the kind that futures were built upon. She'd already been thinking about how to turn in her collar, when she learned Lynch had selected her for his next *favorite*. Cat wanted no part of it. She had never aspired to that exalted role, coveted by so many others in the kink world.

Long after the fact, the beautiful piece of jewelry in her hand now represented a first step toward a future that paralyzed her with fear. Cat doubted she could last even one year as his house slave, let alone two, and his unusual obsession with her made it seem like he would never be done with her. Cat understood now that she'd made her dilemma so much worse by accepting a loan that came with steel strings attached.

She tucked the collar back inside the drawer and went downstairs. It served no purpose to worry. Instead, she'd enjoy the heck out of the Burgundy Rose's claw-foot tub before it ceased to be hers. And since the farmhouse didn't have running water yet after the quake, it was the only way she'd get clean tonight.

Cat locked the farmhouse and walked to the wine house, a bottle of Meadowood wine in her hand and Peanut and Gringo protectively trotting along. The moon was full and she admired the clear cloudless night sky, marveling again that she could see so many more stars here than in the City of Angels. Before she'd taken ten steps her cell buzzed, and she stiffened. Even if it angered Lynch, she wouldn't answer. Not tonight.

But it was Mason. Her heart skittered excitedly, fading her problems to a dull background noise. "Hello," Cat purred breathily, even though she hadn't meant to do her kittenish-thing.

"Hi Fernball. I hope you don't mind my calling so late, but I just wanted to make sure you are okay, after the earthquake and all." His deep masculine voice lacked the dark commanding tone she usually craved, but for once Cat didn't care. Mason's concern warmed her heart...and farther down too.

"That was kind of you, and I'm good. Cleaned up the mess, and I'm ready for business again. Well, once the plumbing's fixed."

"I'm sorry I couldn't get out there today. I needed to finish another project, and now that it's done, I can concentrate on just you."

I like the sound of that!

But he wasn't talking about that kind of attention. "I appreciate it. Really I do."

"Okay then. Glad to hear you're okay. And don't forget our date Friday night, cause I can't wait." He sounded almost boyish with enthusiasm.

"And remember, be ready at seven sharp and looking your dressy best." This time he made it sound like an order, and Cat giggled.

"Yes, sir," she sang. "I'll be ready with bells on." She giggled louder, knowing that Mason had no idea she actually had bells. Pretty, little gold chimers that decorated one of her kinky collars, a matching pink patent leather leash completing the set.

"Good night then," Mason said.

"Good night, sir," she trilled before pushing the button to end the call.

Cat fairly danced the rest of the way and into the wine house. Leaving the dogs outside, she kept the lights off and lit a couple candles. As the tub filled with warm water, she added tons of scented bubble bath before removing her clothes. She poured herself a large glass of chardonnay and took a deep swallow, before setting it down on a nearby table. Tonight, she would pamper herself. Tomorrow, she would worry.

Cat eased into the tub slowly, letting the thick bubbles tease her skin before the warm water enveloped her body. "Mmmmmm."

She gave herself a moment to enjoy the sensation, breathing deeply of the lavender fragrance. She took another long sip of the rich, full-bodied wine, and relaxed back against the wall of the tub. *Heaven!*

The Burgundy Rose was going to be perfect. Her eyes travelled around the room taking in the high ceiling with rough wood beams and raw unfinished walls of quarried stones in shades ranging from sand to ocher. Floor to ceiling curtains framed three smallish windows, the plush velvet in a rich burgundy contrasting wonderfully with the walls. The building was still mostly empty, with only a small table here and a standing lamp there. But when she was done, specialized equipment and thoughtful lighting—designed to cast mysterious shadows or spotlight naked bodies—would turn this space into a magnificent luxury dungeon.

Soon her friends would drive the equipment up from L.A., but she could see it all clearly in her head. Besides the bathroom with sink and toilet, this end held the shower and tub. A Victorian chaise lounge would be strategically placed before both for the client with a voyeur fetish.

Cat grinned, thinking about the look Mason had given her when she'd showed him what she wanted and where, the freestanding glass-walled stall purpose-built for a Dom's viewing pleasure. She'd been able to tell the second Mason's imagination placed her inside the transparent stall, naked with water cascading down her body. She wondered if he might be fantasizing about her in this tub right now.

Cat rested her head against the rim and let her eyes drift shut. She imagined that Mason was in the room with her, watching her bath, watching her lather soap all over her body. Even during the earthquake, she'd been aware of the hard muscle of his arms around her and the press of his solid chest. The scent of him, musky male mixed with clean cotton, and the sound of his soothing voice had helped calm her terror. He wasn't a dominant, of that she was sure, but his strength made her wish he were master of this dungeon. Cat wished that the beautiful crystal collar tucked back in her drawer was his. She would gladly kneel before him to accept it around her neck. She would serve Mason with her mouth and he would claim her body however he chose. As her new Dom, that would be his right. Her pussy clenched, gripping at nothing, wanting him.

Cat moaned.

The sound was loud in the barren silent space. Seeming to bounce off the slate floor and stone walls, it mocked her. Just as Mason would mock her once he learned what she was, what she needed to get off.

Cat sat up abruptly. "Get it through your thick skull. Mason's as vanilla as they come. He's not even French vanilla."

She'd learned over the years to trust her instincts rather than suffer the embarrassment of ridicule or rejection. She'd learned that going it straight was not the answer either. Sooner or later she always grew bored. Usually sooner.

Sighing, she reached between her legs, searching for the plug. She pulled the rubber stopper to let the water drain. The bath had lost its appeal and, anyway, the water was growing cold.

Toweling dry, Cat reminded herself she should not go out with a "vanilla."

Walking home, dogs in attendance, she told herself to cancel Mason's date.

Tucking into bed, Cat admitted to herself that she'd do no such thing. Right or wrong, she would go out with Mason at least once.

After that, well, she'd decide what to do later.

Chapter 6

~ their date has eyes

Mason watched as Cat glanced curiously around the upscale restaurant. He'd been happily doing nothing else all evening.

God, you're pretty!

Every time a new customer came into The Farm Table, she wanted to know if they were tourist or local. Then, if they were local, she wanted to know what they did and if it was related to wine. He cheerfully obliged her, introducing Cat whenever the opportunity arose. Right now she was talking with Felicity Martin, the restaurant's owner, about ways they might cross-promote each other's business and whether the restaurant could cater dinners at the B&B for events or holidays—Christmas at Tulip House and the like.

Mason might have thought it was impressive, how Cat was working so hard to make her B&B the best it could be, but he couldn't seem to think at all.

God, you're pretty!

He couldn't take his eyes off her. Her blond hair was piled up on her head, but wispy strands had escaped to frame her face and tease her neck. He wanted to reach across the table and feel the silk in his fingers. Little flower earrings dangled from her ears, and she wore a fancy, silk dress that floated around her, probably designer. Mason wondered where she found the money for such expensive clothing, but the thought evaporated when he saw how it dipped in front every time she leaned forward, offering tantalizing glimpses of her breasts and a sheer lace bra. That tease of cleavage had kept his eyes dancing downward all evening.

After Cat finished promoting her B&B and choosing a dessert for them to share, she returned her attention to Mason. Her eyes lit when she saw how he was staring at her, and she offered him a stunning smile. He would have sworn in that moment that the earth had stopped spinning, because Cat had become the center of everything. She was sunshine and rainbows and joy made tangible. Mason felt raw pleasure just basking in her glow.

It felt like destiny.

He opened his mouth and all that came out was, "You look very pretty tonight."

Her eyes laughed back to him. "You said that already, twice, but thank you."

"Well you look really great," he huffed.

"I hope you don't mind that I ordered some of the Prager port they carry in stock. I never miss a chance to try local products."

"You did? Somehow I missed that."

Cat laughed again, the sound like effervescent bells on Christmas morning.

"I did," she repeated, "but I don't want you to think I'm trying to get you drunk. Wouldn't be sporting of me."

Mason shook his head, attempting to clear it. "Isn't it usually the guy who tries to get the girl drunk?"

"In my circles, using alcohol is child's play. If you need booze to get a su—"

Cat slammed her mouth shut. "I mean, if you need to get an opponent drunk to get them naked then you're completely lacking in skill."

Mason was out of his element. All this talk of sport and opponents when he knew she was really discussing sex. Maybe he'd drunk too much wine or maybe her innocent freshness— one of the qualities he liked about her—hid darker secrets. Naughty secrets.

His dick went hard faster than a champagne cork explodes from a shaken bottle. He stifled a groan, glad the table hid his dire straits. Then cleared his throat. "Just what all goes on down there in Tinseltown?"

Cat laughed loudly, quite a lot. More than warranted.

Quieting, she replied only, "Oh, you know. Hollywood."

She'd said it as if that explained everything, but Mason wasn't satisfied. If it involved Cat, and getting naked, and having sex, he wanted to hear all there was to know. Everything in fact. "Tell me more. I'm all ears."

But then dessert arrived along with the proprietress. "Do you need anything else," Felicity asked.

Cat's eyes twinkled. "No, I think we're good." She looked at Mason for confirmation.

Not fuckin' likely, he thought.

The rock hard stick trying to poke its way out of his pants told him he wasn't good at all. Or maybe he was very good indeed.

The ladies waited for an answer. "Um, yeah. We're good," he muttered.

They finished the meal mostly in silence. She seemed lost in thought, and Mason was trying desperately to think of any disgusting, gross thing that would lower his staff. All the way would be best, but half-mast would have to do, as the time to stand grew near.

"Thank you for the meal," Cat said rising. "It was delicious."

Mason locked eyes with her, wanting to keep her gaze north of the south pole. He gestured for her to walk ahead of him and he followed, hand to her lower back. Having waited all evening long to touch her, he now had to force the contact to remain casual when he really wanted to caress Cat. Slide his hand lower over the curve of her ass. Slide it up around to her breasts. Slide it all over her body.

He jerked his hand off her back, ostensibly to reach around and open the door.

"It was a pleasure meeting you, Miss Morrison," called Felicity. "I look forward to working with you on a joint event."

"Me too." Cat waved enthusiastically and smiled at Mason as she walked out the door. "What a great place this is. And a wonderful town. I'm going to miss it."

"What?"

"I mean if the B&B doesn't work out."

"It'll be a huge success, you'll see. I'll help too." They stood on the street now, but Mason didn't want to take her home. Wanted more time with her. "Would you like to walk down Main Street? I can show you the sights."

"That'd be great. And, hey, I can't thank you enough for getting the repairs done so quickly, in less than a week. It's great to have running water in the farmhouse again."

"It turned out to be just one fitting that cracked in the quake. The rest of the pipes are sound, I'm sure of that."

"That's good news. So, is it possible we can get the inspector out sooner?"

He'd been avoiding that question all night. Cat looked so hopeful, her eyes wide and eager, and Mason wanted to be her hero, not the man who ruined her dreams. Not tonight.

"I called once and the scheduler said there was nothing she could do, but I'll go there myself on Monday"—he pointed across the street at Town Hall—"and try again."

"Mason, I just don't know what to say. Thank you doesn't seem like enough."

Guilt churned uncomfortably in his gut at her shining adoration. "I have to be honest with you, it doesn't look good. But, I'll give it a shot."

She beamed. "I'm just going to assume it'll work out. At least for tonight anyway."

They started strolling along Main Street, and he pointed out local hotspots. Mason again placed a hand at the base of her back, a part of him just had to connect with her physically. The skin of his palm tingled. The feel of her soft feminine body in his arms after the quake had haunted his dreams. He would never wish for another trembler, but he would go crazy if he didn't get another chance soon to hold Cat, feel her pressed up against him.

As a distraction, Mason focused on digging up tidbits on the town and its colorful citizens. Anything, so he'd stop thinking about getting her naked and doing a little up-close sightseeing.

"Did you know that California's first resort was established here at a mineral springs in 1852, and that two years later an enterprising man named J. Henry Still started the town."

Cat giggled. "You're a regular fount of information, aren't you?"

Shrugging, Mason ignored a stab of embarrassment and admitted, "I looked it up on the internet before I picked you up."

Her glowing smile was enchanting payment. "That was so thoughtful, but if it was founded by Henry Still why's it called St. Helena?"

"This is the ironic part. It's most likely named after the St. Helena Chapter of the Sons of Temperance, founded here in 1854."

"No way."

"It didn't work, obviously, since Krug and others began planting grapes in the 1860's, and wine's been pouring out of here ever since."

"So the wine house on auntie's property could be older than a hundred years. When she and my Uncle Joe bought the place it came with many acres of vineyards, and for many years they liked to make their own wine, just for fun, often selling the surplus grapes. After he passed, she sold off the land to Meadowood Vintners, and that's where she got the funds to remodel the house."

"Yeah, I helped my dad on that project right before I joined the army."

"It saved me a lot of money, because all I needed to do was build my living space in the attic and add two smaller baths to the upstairs bedrooms."

"And a crazy luxury bath into an art studio," he teased.

"Call it artistic license."

They approached two women walking toward them holding hands, and Mason stopped. "Hi, Jen and Tonya. I'd like to introduce you to Cat Morrison. She's opening up a nice Bed and Breakfast just outside of St. Helena. If you ever have too many out of town guests and need a place to put them, they'll find a nice welcome at the Tulip House."

"Nice to meet you. New in town?" asked Tonya, shaking Cat's hand before sliding her arm around the other woman's waist.

"Yes, I—"

"Wait. Is that the old Morrison place?" interrupted Jen. "I remember playing with the chickens there when I was a young child while my gran visited with Mrs. Morrison."

"Yes, she was my aunt."

"I was sorry to hear of her passing a few years ago."

Cat smiled. "I loved the place as a child and it meant a lot that Aunt Tilly left it to me. I'm excited to give a new life to the place, and Mason's doing a wonderful job helping with the renovations."

"Jen and Tonya own a ladies clothing shop over on Madrona Ave."

"Bedroom Bonanza," Jen added, her eyes twinkling, "is not just clothing…"

She broke off to dig in her shoulder bag, so Tonya finished, "Everything we sell is geared toward the bedroom. Fun in the bedroom, if you didn't get my meaning."

Mason felt heat suffuse his face, and elsewhere. "I think she got your meaning, Tonya."

"What? Didn't you like the gift we sent you for your sister's bridal shower?" She leaned in, tone confidential. "It's my newest find. Panties with twinkling LED lights down there to spotlight your—"

"I think she knows what they spotlight," he interrupted.

Next to him, Cat giggled.

Jen handed Cat a small slip of paper. "Here. It's a 10% off coupon we offer all first timers to our store. Come check it out sometime."

"Thanks. It sounds like fun. In fact, I have friends coming up from L.A. next weekend, and I just know *they'll* want those light-up-panties."

"From L.A., huh. I'll show them my sluttiest stuff." Tonya grinned a told-you-so at Mason.

"Say, I just realized," Mason interjected, Tonya is a wiz at social media promotion with thousands of Facebook and YouTube followers for her how-to channel. I'll let you guess what she's how-toing. Anyway, do you think you could put in a good word about Tulip House."

"Hey, I should come out and check out the place." Tonya leaned in eagerly. "Take lots of pictures and post them on my page. Maybe even do a video exposé."

"It'll be fun to see the vineyard after all these years," added Jen.

"Thank you. That would be amazing. Maybe you two could come for brunch sometime, so you can sample the breakfast part of my B&B."

Tonya pulled her cellphone out. "In the meantime, I want a selfie with you so I can post it and start trickling out teasers about your new B&B."

"Sure, of course." Cat watched as Tonya whipped her cell onto a selfie-stick and into position like an Olympic archer in the winning round. She called her over, and Cat hurried to stand between the two women. They smiled up at the camera. After several shots, Tonya swiped through them, seeming satisfied.

"Friend me," she instructed, "and I'll add a link to your B&B's site asap."

"Thank you so much." Cat shook the women's hands again, before making plans for the ladies to brunch at her place.

As they walked away, Cat turned to Mason, giving him a sunny smile. "Thank you for that. Everyone's so friendly around here, it's amazing. So different than L.A."

At the same time, Cat gently touched his forearm, gliding her hand down his bicep. It was just to add emphasis, Mason told himself, but it felt like the most sensual of caresses before she pulled away. He yearned to feel her hands on him again, anywhere. Everywhere.

For what seemed like hours, Mason had been fighting the urge to sweep her into his arms, and he was losing it. They had reached the end of Main Street, and he searched for anyplace that offered a modicum of privacy. Taking her hand, he led her across the street to a small park and drew her under a large tree, out of the light of the street.

In the shadows, he paused, his arm around her waist loosely. He leaned in a little and waited, giving Cat time to pull away, but she didn't. Her eyes dropped to his mouth, and she tilted hers up just the tiniest bit.

God yes!

Mason slid his arms all the way around her and tightened. She came willingly, her body melting against his, though she didn't touch him with her hands. Standing serenely, Cat seemed patient to let him take charge. A surge of testosterone like never before compelled him to go Neanderthal. Throw her over his shoulder and carry her to his cave.

Where the fuck did that come from?

It wasn't how he treated women. Using reserves of will-power Mason hadn't known were in him, he strained to remain the gentleman, even loosening his grip on her a little. Only then, did he lower his mouth and claim her. He brushed his lips over hers in the gentlest of touches and inhaled her wonderful scent. Musky woman and something floral, spicy almost.

Cat moaned into his mouth, and Mason forgot his noble intentions. His tongue plundered the hot recesses of her mouth, fenced with her tongue, and danced victoriously around her lips. His hands laid siege to her body, sweeping low to grab her sweet ass, dragging her against the hard ridge of his erection. She remained still, almost passive, but her impassioned moans urged him onward. He rained kisses down her neck, and one of his hands slid up to cup a breast, grappling and squeezing it. Still Cat didn't move, her sweet supplications the only outward sign that she was as affected as he was.

"Cat," he groaned into her neck. "Touch me. Please."

And like that, Cat joined the dance, her hands sliding up his chest, fondling and testing every inch of him until she grasped handfuls of his hair to pull his mouth back to hers. Then she claimed him, sucking on his tongue before biting his lip, tugging it between her teeth. She flooded his senses. Her whimpers filling his mind. Her fragrant arousal mixed with her perfume scenting the air he breathed. And her taste. *Oh god, her taste!* Tangy port. Delicious honey. He couldn't get enough.

Then Cat ground her hips against his aching dick, her heat branding him. Mason almost lost it.

Groaning, he pulled away and released her. The world tilted and he had to put a hand against the tree trunk.

They both stared at each other, their panting the only sound in the still night air.

Cat looked wonderfully, thoroughly kissed—tousled, dazed, and out of breath. Her mouth opened in the cutest little "Oh" of surprise. Wonder. She brought her hand to her lips and gently touched the swollen skin.

Mason had no idea how he looked to her. Eyes crazed with lust. Or astonished lovesick puppy?

"Damn, that was hot." he muttered. Mason wanted to kiss her again. Like a man starving, she was his sweet succor. But he didn't want to push her too quickly either. Sliding his fingers through his hair, he asked, "How about if I show you the shops on the other side of the street."

"Of course, sir. Whatever you desire." There was that strangely sexy Cat again—soft, compliant, breathy—a quality she seemed capable of turning on and off as easily as one flips a light switch. He liked that Cat, very much!

Her cell buzzed in her purse and he waited for her to fish it out, but she ignored it as they walked across the street.

Mason's hand immediately returned to her lower back. He was drawn to connect with her as if she were gravity itself and he, like everything else in the universe, unable to resist the pull. "And Newton thought he discovered it."

"I'm sorry, sir, could you repeat that." Her tone remained silky, her expression dreamy.

"It was nothing. Just me mumbling."

Her phone buzzed again and then immediately after started ringing.

Again, Cat ignored it.

"Maybe you should answer that," Mason suggested. "I don't mind waiting."

Cat nodded and he stepped away, while she retrieved her cell. She didn't attempt to answer it but her demeanor shifted the instant she saw who was calling. From dreamy to anxious as quickly as the flip of another switch. Turning away slightly, she swiped at her phone to read the texts, and Mason saw her entire body stiffen, go from soft and sexy to rigid and scared. Her head popped up, and her gaze swung from left to right as if searching for something.

"What is it?" Mason stepped up to her, his hand slipping back to her waist.

"It's nothing." Cat sidled out of his light hold and strode down the sidewalk, tucking her phone back in her purse. She continued to dart glances about as if something or someone was about to jump out from behind a bush.

Mason hurried forward and matched her brisk pace. "Something in that text upset you. I know it's none of my business, but if there's anything I can do." Whatever it was, he wanted to comfort her, his hand already reaching to Cat, but he stopped himself just inches from her back.

"Could you please take me home now?"

Mason immediately agreed and walked her to his pickup. During the brief drive, neither of them spoke, Cat clearly distracted by the text. She didn't wait for him to open the truck door for her and was halfway to the front porch before he'd turned off the engine and emerged. It was obvious he wouldn't get an invitation inside, but he still wanted to make sure she was all right.

"It's okay. You don't need to escort me to my door. I'll be fine." And to prove it, Peanut and Gringo appeared out of nowhere to stand at her side. Mason followed her up anyway.

"Cat, I hope it wasn't anything I did? If I kissed you too soon, I'm sorry."

"No!" That had got her attention. "Don't say that. I loved the kiss, truly."

"Well that's a relief. Hate to think I'd lost my touch," he joked, trying to lighten the mood. He leaned in to give her another one, something quick, wanting to end their night on a good note.

Cat jerked back. Even raised her hands in front of her, warding him off. That bothered him. He'd never forced himself on a woman in his life. "Cat, I—"

"It's not you. You're great. It's me. All my fault." She turned away to punch the code into the lock. "Thank you again for dinner and good night."

Mason couldn't leave. Something wasn't right. "Cat, wait!"

Just inside the door, she turned back. "Look. I think it's better if we keep our relationship professional. It's for the best." Then Cat pulled the door closed in his face.

There were only two options—pound on the door or leave. So Mason turned away, heading for his truck, but questions pounded in his head. *What had the text said? Why did she seem so scared and what had she been looking for as they walked down Main Street?*

Concern made him turn back to the farmhouse, planning to bang on the door until he got answers, but two low growls coming from the top of the porch stopped him. The dogs knew him well, always wagged their tails and begged for a scratch, but somehow they understood he wasn't welcome now. He could see their bared teeth and realized there was no getting past them, not tonight.

Defeated, he returned to the truck and drove home. Those questions were going to make him crazy. And the biggest thing he wanted to know was, *what had he done wrong?* That would keep him up all night.

Chapter 7

~ a wicked barn-raising

It was Friday late morning and Cat listened eagerly for the sound of cars coming down the driveway. Even with her troubles and the guilt she felt about what had happened with Mason, she couldn't stop the excitement that bubbled inside at seeing her old gang. The dogs barked and she ran out to look, but only twittering birds greeted her.

She had avoided Mason all week. Easy to do now that his work at Tulip House was completed. He'd called and texted many times, asking how she was, but Cat had only responded once, thanking him and repeating her request to keep things professional. But she missed him. Remorse and regret had competed for prominence over the past six days.

Cat had replayed that night in her mind over and over, searching for a different solution. She'd long since deleted the text from her Dom, but the words were emblazoned permanently in her brain...

"What are you doing kissing another man when you belong to me?"

Lynch had shocked her, scared her, made her nearly retch right there on Main Street. She was grateful still that she'd made it home before her dinner came back out.

After hearing nothing more from Mason for a few days, she'd received an email this morning, very professional, which was good. Just didn't feel good. And it was disappointing news—the inspection could not be moved forward. She was grateful for his efforts on this, which only added to her guilt about shutting him out without an explanation.

But, what else could she do?

For her sake, and for Mason's too, Cat would keep her distance from "the hired help," as Lynch had called him. She was doubly grateful Mason had finished working on her place, because it meant that the two men would never meet. She wasn't sure how either guy would handle it. She wished Lynch wasn't coming, had tried again to suggest it in an email, but that had made her Dom angrier. And he was really, *really* angry.

She had called Sir back immediately once Mason had dropped her at home. She'd tried to make light of it, the kiss hadn't meant anything she told him, but Lynch had been furious. Unwilling to discuss it, he made it clear that he'd address it in person. On her person. Lynch also refused to answer her question: "How did you know?" but she had to assume he was watching her somehow. The idea that he'd hired someone to follow her frightened Cat even more than the discipline that was coming, probably coming tomorrow night.

Her gut clenched, as did a part of her body farther south. She was a pain slut and the idea of a punishment always aroused. But she felt something new too—violent distaste. After everything she'd gone through, hiding who she was from her family, suffering years of thinking she was a perv, Cat suddenly wished that she were in fact different. Wished that the image of a crop whipping across her ass didn't make her body fire in anticipation.

Wished that life with a great guy like Mason would be enough for her. For the first time, Cat wished that she was...normal.

She stared out the window, unseeing, knowing that she wasn't and never would be normal, at least not in the bedroom.

Honk! Honk! Honk!

Peanut and Gringo barked with gusto and raced to greet the newcomers. Cat sprinted out the door, adding her voice to the cacophony.

"Hi!" she called, waving excitedly from the porch.

And she let herself forget it all in the joyous commotion as her four friends piled out of two vehicles, a sedan and a pickup, both of which were loaded down with large boxes. They didn't wait for their turn but jumbled together into a giant hug, laughing and talking at once, before Sam, her oldest buddy, lifted her up and swung her around.

"Man, I've missed you," said the young man, squeezing the air from her lungs with his enthusiasm. He had surfer-dude hair and a carefree attitude to match.

"We caravanned as you can see," announced Sady, a tall, strong, beautiful black woman who radiated authority. "I *even* let Sam *drive.*" She tapped him on the shoulder. "Let Cat go now and give the rest of us a chance."

Immediately, he dropped his arms and stepped back, eyes downcast, his insouciance replaced by deference.

Cat snorted, her laughing eyes darting between the two of them. "So that's how it is?"

"Sam's former Domme finally released him, and I snatched him up." Sady wrapped Cat into a big bear hug. "Missed you girl."

Standing quietly, Sam peeked up at Cat and ventured, "I did make Mistress work for it." His hand absentmindedly caressed an elaborately-carved leather collar around his neck.

"Played hard to get," reported Gotham, the other guy in their gang of four, as he took his turn hugging Cat.

Sady grinned. "Yes, but I got my revenge on Sam. I *played* him hard. Then I collared him."

"She's not called Mistress *Sady* for nothing," rejoined Sam, referring to her nickname, Sady the Sadistic, while rubbing his butt for comic effect. Everyone laughed, but a warning glance from Sady had Sam shutting his mouth.

"Where's your collar?" Gotham asked Cat, censure ringing loud in his tone. In a black t-shirt and black jeans the look was bland enough, but his powerful presence would let anyone know that he was a Master, anyone familiar with kink, at least.

Cat's hand flew to her bare neck. "Oh! I forgot."

"Master Lynch will be here tomorrow morning. I suggest you wear it."

"Yes, Sir. Thank you for reminding me." Cat was grateful that Lynch would never deign to drive eight hours, choosing instead to fly up and rent a car. It gave her the rest of the day to enjoy the company of her friends as their equal. Well almost equal.

Gotham wasn't her Dom but he was still a dominant. He'd always been a friend and sometimes teacher to her. And Gotham wasn't his real name. He had three in total—his Dom moniker, a stage name, and his real one that no one knew. Good-looking and well-built, he was a stunt double by day and a master for hire by night.

His own sub, bursting with eagerness for her turn, stood obediently behind Gotham, waiting for permission. The vivacious redhead was younger than Cat by nearly ten years, and her youthful exuberance could at times get her into trouble.

Gotham looked over his shoulder. "Pet, aren't you going to hug your friend?"—his voice tinged with disapproval. It was his special brand of evil kink. Punish for acting without permission. Reprimand for not acting quickly enough. Which meant he was always punishing, but clearly Pet was thriving. Squealing with delight, she danced forward and latched onto Cat, kissing her cheek and holding her tight.

Then Pet surprised her. Putting her mouth at Cat's ear, she whispered a warning. "Master Lynch is really angry with you."

"I know," Cat replied quietly. The weight of her problems felt heavier and more restrictive than any physical bondage she'd ever faced in a dungeon. It threatened to ruin the gift of a carefree afternoon with her friends, so she pushed a smile to her face.

"Come inside. I've got lunch ready."

* * *

Three hours later Cat brushed her hair out of her eyes with the back of her hand and looked around the inside of the Burgundy Rose, taking in all they'd accomplished.

"Thanks, Pet," she said accepting the glass of cold lemonade the sub had made back at the farmhouse. They'd all been working hard assembling the equipment that would turn the empty space into a dungeon.

"Thank you guys so much!" she told the gang. "I expected the work to take all weekend, and I think we'll get it done by midday tomorrow."

"You know I wouldn't miss this for anything," Sam replied from where he was helping Gotham hang chains and pulleys from hooks in the ceiling's crossbeam. "I was the one who introduced you to this world, remember, and now you own your own dungeon!"

"An unbelievably fantastic one," murmured Pet, staring in awe at everything and then twirling over to the BDSM bed positioned against the far wall.

"Do you like it?" Sam asked Cat. "Lynch wanted us to surprise you with it."

"Oh, it was a surprise all right." Cat took in the outrageously expensive, steel-framed canopy bed. Of course, she *liked* it. How could she not? It was the exact model she'd wanted but rejected due to its four-thousand-dollar price. She hadn't realized that he'd known about it.

"It's perfect," she replied, knowing they awaited her answer. But Cat wished it didn't feel like one more entry on the liability side of her account with Lynch.

"I love it too!" sang the vivacious Pet. Dancing about the massive structure, she announced, "I *want* Master Gotham to hang me from it and beat me silly."

"Pet!"

Instantly, the room went silent, all eyes on Gotham's sub.

Pet's gaze dropped to the floor. Realizing her monumental gaff, her body went down next, landing to kneel at his feet. She moved into Gotham's preferred presentation pose and whispered, "I'm sorry, Master."

Gotham didn't state the obvious—that bottoms didn't make demands of their betters. "Until you can learn appropriate discourse, I'd suggest you remain silent." His phrasing didn't fool anyone. It wasn't a suggestion.

Pet nodded her understanding, ready to remain on the cold stone floor for as long as he wished.

Gotham smiled down at her, his hand petting her head. "Now, how about you help Sam and I test the suspension system. It's rock solid, but I'd like to check out the various configurations with a live body."

For Gotham, this was an uncharacteristic kindness, and Pet jumped excitedly to her feet. She gestured to her top, pulling the sleeve off her shoulder.

"Yeah. Take it all off. Might as well test the padding on the cuffs while we're at it."

Without a second's hesitation, Pet stripped in front of everyone. Like Cat and Sam and other subs, modesty had been trained out of her, replaced by pride in her naked body. Leaving them to it, Cat mused that it was one of the blessings of the kink world that no matter one's size, shape, or age—anyone could be a sexual being and everyone counted.

"Cat, come help me put the spanking bench together," ordered Sady, standing next to an unopened box. Except for the St. Andrew's Cross, the rest was done. There was a table with a cage underneath next to two chairs by the potbelly stove, ensuring heat if not comfort for any imprisoned sub. A restraining platform that could double as a massage table stood in one corner, and a throne on a dais was prominently front and center, ensuring that whoever ruled from the chair could survey the entire dungeon.

"Yes, Mistress." Cat hurried over with the box cutter in her hand.

"So I see you followed Gotham's suggestion." Sady pointed at her neck, before taking the knife and slicing through the cardboard.

"Yeah, I haven't worn it in two months, so figured I'd better get used to it again."

"I wondered if you'd been to any of the San Francisco clubs?"

"No, beside the fact that Master Lynch wouldn't approve of my going, I don't know anyone in the local scene, yet. And now after the earthquake delayed my opening, I really need to stay in his good graces if I hope to get some kind of concession from him."

Cat stood by, helping the Domme like a nurse assists a doctor. Sady systematically removed each bar and padded piece, and Cat laid them out on the floor in an orderly fashion.

Speaking *sotto voce*, Sady probed, "I'd wondered if everything was okay, after you implied that you might miss your first payment. I know that he was your last resort, but I'm sad that you've left yourself vulnerable. He's not a concession-y type of Master, and he doesn't accept mistakes."

"I know, but it was an earthquake, for fuck's sake."

"Cat!" Sady wasn't *her* mistress, but she didn't tolerate any sub swearing in her presence.

"Sorry. It's just that the quake was something totally out of my hands. The repairs have been completed in record time, and the only thing holding me up is getting the inspector back out here. I have this one weekend to convince Master that I can run this business before he takes it away."

"Hold the seat in place while I screw it to the base," Sady instructed.

Cat did as she was told, an innate reaction to authority—male or female—something she knew would make her feminist take-charge mother cringe.

Sady eyed Cat speculatively. "You do know that your *managerial* skills are not the real issue."

Cat nodded. "That is just his excuse to force my subjugation."

"It's not for nothing that he's made it big in Hollywood. Lynch has turned manipulation and risk-taking into an art form. Arranging people like pawns and gambling with fortunes. And now he's maneuvered you right where he wants you."

"And I let him. I know it's my fault."

Sady reached out and caressed Cat's shoulder, offering comfort. "It's not about fault, but I am worried about you."

"There has to be a way to convince him to give me more time, and I'm going find it."

Sady did not looked convinced.

The rest of the day was pure bliss. They ate dinner on the big porch and spent hours catching up. By virtue of his higher status, Gotham would be the first to break in the dungeon. Shortly after dinner, he ordered Pet to the Burgundy Rose to prepare for him. He invited them to watch, but only Sam took him up on it…with Sady's permission, of course.

"It'll give us time to catch up, girlfriend," Sady told Cat, squeezing her hand and winking.

"I'd like you to try some wine I discovered from nearby Meadowood Vintners." At her friend's nod, Cat said, "I'll be right back."

Inside, she opened the bottle and checked her messages. Lynch had texted he'd be delayed, wouldn't arrive until around six the next day and to have dinner ready for him. She wanted to text back: *Make your own damn dinner!* Instead, she replied in the affirmative and that she was—*argh!*— looking forward to his arrival.

It was yet one more indication that Catriona Fern Morrison, happy sexual submissive by night, would never last as a docile servant by day. While she had submissive tendencies during sex and might even defer to a dominant's authority out of the bedroom, Cat could never give up her freewill and allow someone else complete control over her, not even on a temporary basis. It just wasn't who she was, but Lynch wouldn't accept that she wasn't a 24/7 lifer.

Returning to the porch, she handed Sady a glass with just a taste of the wine and waited. Her friend was a connoisseur, and Cat wanted her opinion.

Sady did all the usual things. Sniffing. Gazing and swirling. Then, holding the glass to her lips, she took a small sip and smiled. "Delicious." She held out the glass for it to be filled. "Meadowood, you said?"

Cat joined her on the wooden swing and filled her own glass, then handed the bottle to her friend.

"Private Reserve Northern Red," Sady said, reading the label. "I'll have to pick up some bottles before heading back. You know I like to stock unusual, hard-to-get varieties."

"Yeah, and this is virtually impossible to get. The vintner, Sal Moretti, has sold most of this year's stock to brokers and collectors, but he does have some bottles here for local clientele.

I'll call Sal and let him know you're stopping by." Cat grinned. "We're going to do some cross-promotion, so I've got an in."

"For a sub, you're certainly quite a mover and shaker, but I'm happy for you." Sady lifted her glass in salute.

"To moving and shaking…in life and, more importantly, in the bedroom or dungeon." Laughing, they clinked their glasses.

"Speaking of sex. Tell me about this plumber of yours?"

Sady's question surprised her. "What? How do you know about him?"

"The whole L.A. gang knows."

"No. Please tell me you're kidding."

"Sorry, sweet kitty cat. Lynch was hosting one of his showcase dinners for the collaring of his newest girl, the one who's supposed to replace you as day slave when you move into Lynchland."

"*If* I move in."

"Yeah, well, that is the question, isn't it? Anyway, Lynch exploded when he found out you'd gone out with your plumber and that you kissed him. He took out his fury on every girl in his harem."

This can't be happening! No matter the fact that she'd tried to break it off with Lynch, let him know gently that she didn't want to be his sub anymore, he would see her behavior as a betrayal—of him and his authority, and it had all played out before an audience. No wonder he was so angry. It also explained how Pet knew to warn her. Cat's pulse raced and she felt suddenly ill. She closed her eyes and counted silently to ten, breathing deep with each beat in a centering technique Lynch had taught her.

"Catriona. It's okay. It's not the eighteenth century and slavery's illegal. Lynch can scare you but he can't really force you."

"Yes, but it might mean walking away from Tulip House."

"Do you really like this plumber of yours?"

"He's not my plumber. Not my anything. We went out to dinner one time. That's all."

"But he did kiss you, right?"

Cat nodded.

"Did you like it?" Sady's authoritative tone made clear she expected an answer to the personal question.

Cat thought about lying, but she was a friend and could be trusted. "It was…*wonderful*. Amazing. But you can't tell Master Lynch I said that. And, anyway, it will never happen again."

"Why not? You have to settle things with Lynch, but then you deserve to have a great lover. We all do." Sady laughed, a deep rich sound in the silent night air.

Cat snorted. "If Mason, the nice guy, ever found out what I'm really like, he'd run for the hills, straight up those pretty grapevine lined rows until he's far away from perverted, kinky, wicked, lil 'ol me."

"You never really know until you know." Sady gave her a sly wink.

"*Sady!*" Cat was exasperated. "Have you seen sweet, pristine St. Helena with its fancy wine bars and doggie day spas and organic cheese shops? It's Nice Town, U.S.A., and Mason should be its mayor."

"You'd be surprised at the kink that goes on behind closed doors in pretty little towns across this country."

"I really can't imagine any universe where Mason Steele dons a black leather vest and chains me from the ceiling so he can whip me silly."

Sady raised an eyebrow. "Over the years, I've met too many mild-mannered kitten-men who change stripes and extend their claws once they're in the bedroom."

Cat quietly shook her head, but didn't reply.

"Now, if you'll excuse me, I'd better go check on my sub. Sam can get quite worked up watching others play, and I've a mind to let him to expend some of that energy on me." She grinned. "Thanks for inviting us and giving me the use of your beautiful master suite."

"It's the least I could do, after you all are helping so much."

Sady left her then and, humming to herself, walked down the dark lane toward the dungeon.

Cat realized the soundproofing must work well, because she'd heard no spanking sounds or searing shrieks from the Burgundy Rose. She knew Gotham, and he wouldn't spare the rod, not even if it spoiled his Pet silly.

Cat rocked slowly on the hanging bench, thinking over their conversation.

Sady had said that Mason might surprise her, might discover that he liked to wield more than power tools. "I wish," Cat murmured, hugging her knees. She'd happily become his sex kitten in a red-hot minute.

But deep inside, instinct told her that Mason would be stunned, probably disgusted, if he ever learned what went on behind *her* closed doors. Even if they had fun in the vanilla sack for a while, Cat knew from past experience that eventually she'd want it dark and dirty. The emotional pain and disappointment were never worth the initial fun.

* * *

The next morning, the bottoms provided the food and the tops the labor, finishing the dungeon by noon. They decided to eat lunch in St. Helena, and Cat took them to The Farm Table. Afterwards they strolled through town, and it was her turn to point out the sights. And, of course, everyone bought something risqué from the Bedroom Bonanza, although only Pet wanted the light-up lingerie. "Perfect for the holidays," she quipped.

Leaving the store, Cat wondered if her new friends, Jen and Tonya, would be a source of referrals for dungeon rentals, maybe even want to be customers by the looks of some the merchandize they carried. But their connection to Mason made it messy. Either they'd tell him about her secret or she'd put them in a position of keeping secrets from their old friend. Cat sighed. It would be so much easier if Mason were in on her secret—but then she might lose her closest St. Helena friend. He seemed too straight up to approve of her kink.

Returning to Tulip House by midafternoon, Cat and Pet made dinner. Sam played fetch with Peanut and Gringo, and the tops surprised Cat by offering to work on the rose garden, which had been partly destroyed in the effort to fix the broken pipe.

After two hours of toiling outside, Cat brought Gotham and Sady cold lemonade and surveyed her newly replanted rose bushes. "Wow! Thanks so much. I just didn't have time to get to it yet."

Gotham grinned. "You know I like to get down and dirty," he joked, although in reality it wasn't a joke. "The plants should recover nicely, and you'll have blooms next spring."

She hugged them both before returning to the kitchen. Cooking wasn't her strong suit, but she'd been perfecting her "breakfasts" since that would be the only meal she'd serve guests at the B&B. Tonight they'd feast on her favorite recipes, from mushroom quiche to apple sausage to almond tarts, and all made with local ingredients.

An hour later, the two subs were setting the table and Cat was finishing dinner when she heard the roar of a powerful engine. Thinking it was Mason's truck, her stomach tightened and her hands shook slightly. She hurried to the door ready to send him on his way. So, she actually felt relief when an unfamiliar sports car pulled up with Lynch behind the wheel. Cat quickly turned back to swipe his collar from the counter where she'd tossed it earlier. She wasn't that kind of sub—the 24/7 cooking, cleaning, and acting-like-a-servant kind, but for the rest of the weekend she'd pretend she was to get on Lynch's good side.

In truth, the only *service* she enjoyed involved a lot of kneeling and sucking and stroking and…basically anything to do with ecstasy, hers or her lover's. However, now was not the time to stand on principle—her future was more important. Cat quickly cinched the collar around her neck and plastered a pleasant expression over the grimace that threatened to reveal her true feelings.

She hurried out to the porch and smiled and tried to look happy as she walked toward him, chin high, searching his face for signs of anger. Lynch just watched her silently, his eyes calculating.

Cat lowered herself to kneel before him on the cement, and from her subservient position invited him into her home. "Hi, Sir. Welcome to Tulip House."

Staring up at him, she waited while he scrutinized the grounds. He'd been there before when she'd first inherited it, and he was clearly taking in the improvements. New paint. Porch swing. Two dogs that came forward to sniff his leg. Cat opened her mouth to warn them off.

"Sit." Lynch's powerful voice worked on strange dogs too, it seemed, because their butts hit the ground.

Gringo turned his head to look at Cat kneeling next to him, and she could have sworn he was asking if the guy towering over them met with her approval.

"Good boy," she praised quietly. "He's a...*friend.*"

"You've done a good job here," he said.

Lynch bent down and took hold of her forearms, hauling her up to stand before him, so he could inspect her too. She'd worn his favorite dress, applied makeup, and styled her hair the way he liked. She stood passively, as she'd been trained, and let him turn her so he could examine her backside. When Lynch pulled her back around to face him, he was smiling. "It's good to see you again, Miss Pussy."

He pulled her into a big hug, holding her tight and burying his face in her hair, and she let him. Her Dom clearly cared for her, in his own way.

"Dinner is ready, Sir." It was the gentlest of nudges, but it worked.

"Great. I'm starved." He waved as the gang assembled. "Hey, everybody. Thanks for the hard work on our dungeon. Can't wait to see it. And I brought champagne. We're celebrating," he proclaimed.

Cat marveled that Lynch didn't seem angry with her. Nor did he seem annoyed or fatigued from hours of travelling, but instead he was relaxed as if he'd spent the afternoon working out his demons on one of his subs. Relief flooded her that maybe this visit would go well and she'd get what she needed from him.

Over dinner, Lynch ruled, as he always did, being larger than life and gregarious. He graciously allowed the subs to sit at the table, a rare treat in his presence. He was old-school Hollywood but with a kinky new-school twist. He was Master Lynch, no pseudonym needed because no one dared risk exposing him and being blackballed—career balls or actual ones. Rumors abounded about what went on behind the tall walls of his estate, but that only added to his mystique. It helped that no one set foot inside without handing over their phones and other electronics, and signing a non-disclosure agreement. A few early lawsuits proved he could bring anyone to their knees for breaking his confidence, so no one did.

As a result, Robert Lynch lived the life he wanted and everyone, kinky or not, vied for his notice or approval and especially for a coveted invitation to Lynchland. The place had two hundred feet of ocean front, two pools, hot-tubs, and everything else needed for a *very* good time, including, of course, his playroom and the vaunted house-slave. Depending on his mood, *it* was reserved for his exclusive use or available to all— along with mandatory condoms, of course.

His stable of subs came just for parties or private sessions but didn't live in. They spent the majority of their time at Lynchland as servants or playthings in his version of a "red room of pain." Styled like a glorious pasha's harem, all iridescent silks and plush recliners, the dungeon held every type of BDSM apparatus and toys imaginable. It took up the entire top floor of his large mansion with floor to ceiling windows overlooking the ocean. It was the most exclusive perk and privilege for any guest, requiring yet another NDA and the promise of a return "favor" at some future time.

Lynch's parties were his kinky take on Hugh Hefner's lifestyle, and one never knew who might be there—from business leaders to movie directors to the occasional royal kinkster from overseas. Cat had enjoyed the heck out of it, from walking the movie-premiere red carpet in designer dresses to playing all night long in the dungeon, but she'd also seen firsthand what happens when a sub was promoted to house slave. For some reason, the generous pasha turned tyrant after a woman gave him *all* her power. Once he took their incredible gift of freedom and service, Lynch soon ceased to value the person, lending *it* to his powerful friends, treating *it* like furniture.

Cat wished she'd never been swept up in the excitement of his rich lifestyle. The trips and parties, gifts and clothes had become a burden as his demands of her increased. Her escape had been her job at the Malibu Inn, but he had grown possessive of her time, pressuring her to quit and move in with him. He'd hinted that her role as house slave would be different from others, but Cat didn't want it any way it came.

As the animated conversation continued—even Pet had been given permission to talk—one thing became clear. Most likely it was the reason Lynch was acting so nicely to everyone. He assumed he'd already won, that it was just a matter of time until Cat was "it." The prospect choked her, like a noose tightening around her neck. She slid a surreptitious finger inside the leather band circling her throat, pulling at it, but Master's collar would never again feel comfortable on her.

After dinner, her friends wanted to go downtown to try out Sippity Doo Dah, a quaint little wine bar they'd discovered earlier in the day.

Cat was torn between not wanting to run into anyone she knew with Lynch there and wanting to put off the retribution that she knew was coming, even if he hadn't given the slightest hint that he was still angry. But Master found it amusing to toy with his sub's equilibrium, playing the feline and rodent game until his quarry was jittery and tense. Since she'd already made the mistake of taking his cheese, Lynch had her cornered, and it would only increase his pleasure to watch her squirm until he was finally ready to pounce.

For that reason, she was finding it hard to enjoy the evening. They sat at the front of the nightspot on a grouping of comfortable sofas. Lynch was indulging Cat's interest in local wine, so she could taste more of her neighbor's products. And with a growing tab, the friendly owner, known locally as Quick Pour Lenore, was giving them the VIP treatment. It wasn't just that they were big spenders—extraordinarily big, thanks to Cat's Dom—but the owner had recognized Robert Lynch. Her fawning, making it clear Lenore knew he was a Hollywood bigwig. One good tweet from him and every tourist in town would flock to her establishment.

"So here's another Napa Ranch merlot that I'd just love to get your opinion on. Try it on the house." Lenore hurried around, pouring everyone a sample. "It pairs well with pears and strawberries and a mellow cheese."

"Very nice," Lynch pronounced. "Leave the bottle and add it to my tab." Lenore beamed.

He turned to Cat seated next to him. "I'd have ordered the cheese plate, but after your delicious cooking, I'm stuffed."

Praise too? Cat tried to look suitably pleased by his compliment as the gang reiterated their appreciation for the meal. Maybe he really wasn't angry with her after all.

"Thank you." Dropping to a whisper in public, she added the requisite, "Sir."

Later, she and Pet excused themselves to the restroom. While they washed hands, the young girl watched her curiously. "I guess I was wrong about Master Lynch being angry. He seems *totally* infatuated with you." Awe of him and envy of Cat filled her voice.

"No, I think he probably is angry. Just doesn't like to tip his hand, and I appreciate the heads-up."

"It's not my business, Miss Pussy, but—"

"Call me Cat."

"Okay. I hope you won't mind my asking, Miss Cat, but I don't understand your behavior. Is it to make Master Lynch jealous?"

Finished drying her hands, Cat threw the paper towel into the trash. "What do you mean?"

"I would give anything to be Master Gotham's live-in, if he kept one. And any sub would jump at the chance to become *your* Master's house slave. So I don't see why you'd risk everything to go on a date with a...a *vanilla?*" Distaste etched her tone and shaped her face into a pout.

Cat stared at the sweet girl that she'd always found fun to be around. She was so young it made her feel old. Cat didn't know what to say. It was true. Being Lynch's live-in was the pinnacle of L.A.'s kink scene. It opened doors and transformed lives. More than one movie star had gotten her break thanks to being his house girl. Others had been able to go to college on his parting generosity. But Lynch's interest in her felt different. Those women were all total natural submissives and had wanted the honor. She wasn't and didn't. Even more than that, Lynch's obsession with her went way beyond anything she'd seen before. Cat wasn't sure he'd ever let her go, were she to agree to his demands.

"It's complicated. Lynch and I...it's different between us." Cat wasn't sure Pet would understand or agree, so she left it at that.

"Miss Cat, I don't want to offend you, but I just think you should also know that you're upsetting your old friends."

They had turned to go, but Cat stopped, unease crawling up her spine. "Why? What's going on down there?"

"Well, the current house slave is tired of waiting for you to take her place. Miss Aphrodite has served more than two years and wants her reward. She's already picked out a fancy sports car. And there's a handsome new Dom in town that Master Lynch has promised he'd give her to."

Cat nodded. It was unfortunate that the girl was caught in the middle, but she'd agreed to the standard contract—and the stipulation that she serve *until* a replacement was trained. "I'm sorry for Aphrodite, of course, but it's not really my problem."

Pet's tight face suggested she didn't agree. "Also, the rest of his stable is either jealous or say that you're a snob, thinking you're too good to take your turn. And they're angry because while you dawdle up here, their words, they've all been on the receiving end of Master Lynch's frustration with you."

"Oh! I didn't know." Cat felt bad for the subs. She didn't mean for them to suffer, even the ones who'd been jealous and catty in the past. "I'm sorry about that. Really I am."

She walked back to the table lost in thought. The men all stood when they rejoined the group, one of Lynch's codes of gentlemanly behavior that had originally drawn her to him.

"I ordered a bottle of that NoCal Private Reserve once I saw they carried it," Sady said. "I told everyone they'd love it."

Before Cat could take her place on the couch between Lynch and Sam, she heard her name called.

"Cat?"

No! Please no.

But Mason's voice was unmistakable. Pivoting slowly, she plastered a casual smile on her face. "Hi, um…Mr. Steele."

He looked at her oddly, but she couldn't tell him that it was another of Master Lynch's codes of civility—subs in his presence always spoke respectfully to men. She glanced helplessly down at Sady, but the Domme was looking with interest at the newcomer.

Everyone stared at Mason, but when she glanced at Lynch, he'd risen to stand next to her, his dark expression cynical and calculating. She could hardly breathe as the two men sized each other up.

"I'm Robert Lynch." He took the upper hand. "And you must be the…plumber." With just a faint inflection, Lynch made it sound utterly distasteful, like Mason shoveled shit for a living.

Mason jerked back slightly, then forced a tight smile. Sticking his hand out, he said, "Nice to meet you…*Bob.*"

Cat gasped and Pet giggled.

Gotham shushed his sub while the others pretended great interest in their wine.

Cat tried to hide her skyrocketing admiration of Mason. Somehow he'd known just how to take Lynch's subtle gauntlet and slap it back across his face, because nobody *ever* called the Master…Bob.

"Sit, Bastet," Lynch ordered.

Mortified, Cat felt her face blossom red, but she obeyed, sitting down on the couch.

Mason was transfixed by their interaction, his face puzzled, and she wanted him to stop staring at her like that.

She had to say something to break the tension. "These are my friends from Los Angeles," she chirped, embarrassment making her tone reedy. Taking a breath, she tried again. "I'll introduce—"

"We're all very close," Lynch interrupted, settling back down and putting his arm possessively around her shoulders.

Cat watched helplessly as Mason stared at them, taking it all in. Then his eyes slid over to meet hers, and she saw hurt there, before they swept to take in the rest of the group. He paused for a moment at the collar around Pet's neck. It was a pretty thing and almost looked like a piece of jewelry. When his eyes settled on the obvious dog collar around Sam, complete with a large metal loop for a leash, his eyes flared and Mason leaned forward a tad for a better look.

Watching his intense scrutiny, Cat realized what would happen next and wanted to cover her throat with her hand. Slowly, his eyes trailed back in search of her neck and he stared.

Cat raised her chin and gazed defiantly back at him. She could almost see the confusion churning his mind as he tried to work it out. At least she wore a pretty choker, having refused early on to wear an obvious dog collar in public. When Lynch had presented her with the gold necklace, studded with semi-precious stones, she'd agreed to the compromise.

Mason's eyes lifted to hers. They burned with questions. Almost as if he were speaking to himself, still working things out, he muttered, "I couldn't understand what happened the other night…but that must be why you…" Mason trailed off when he saw her subtly shake her head, panic roaring through her.

Lynch stood up again, facing off against the other man. "Why…*what?* What is it you want to know about my su—" Lynch snapped his mouth shut, respecting Cat's longstanding request for privacy among the straight set. "…about my girlfriend?"

Cat shook her head harder from the sofa and silently willed Mason to let it go. His gaze flicked back and forth between the two of them. "Nothing," he muttered. "It was nothing. Nice to meet you all."

He turned and walked out of the wine shop empty handed. Cat wanted to chase after him. Tell him how much she adored him. Beg him for a second chance. She tracked Mason with her eyes as he walked past the windows, drinking him up, wanting every last drop till she couldn't see him anymore. And still she gazed after where he had been.

Cat slowly became aware that everyone was looking at her. Still standing, Lynch's eyes drilled into her, suspicion making them narrow.

He was definitely angry now. "This party's over," he pronounced.

The gang seemed to agree. The festive mood gone, replaced by a sullen cloud as they stood and gathered their things.

Lynch dropped a wad of cash on the table. "My treat."

A chorus of thank you's erupted, before silence again descended and they made their way outside.

Lenore rushed over as they exited, her profuse thanks following them out the door.

With brutal strength, Lynch gripped Cat's elbow, forcing them to lag behind.

In a harsh whisper, he delivered the sentence she'd been dreading but expecting all evening. "We're now going to spend some quality time together, so I can teach you not to cheat on me. By morning, I promise that your body won't let you forget to whom you belong."

There was a time when his threats had been a fun part of their game. When she tingled at the thought of his pain-filled lessons.

That time was long gone.

* * *

In too short a time they were all back inside the farm-house. It was amazing how her Dom ruled without saying much, even over the other dominants. Earlier in the day, they'd all offered to stand by her, but she told them it wasn't necessary. None of them knew the full extent of her deal with Lynch, and for as long as possible she would keep from them her secret shame.

"It's fine," she had reassured. "You know us. We like to play it hot and cold."

Sady had snorted, responding, "I don't know about that, because the only thing that's going to be hot tonight is your ass. Flaming cherry red hot."

Her friends had laughed. This was their kinky world after all.

So now that it was time, no one interfered. As if actors in a play, they murmured their lines of goodnight and faded away to their assigned suites. Sam following Sady. Pet following Gotham. Each giving her small reassuring smiles.

Gotham went so far as to whisper in her ear, "Are you sure?" and Cat nodded. This was her mess and enough people were already hurting because of it.

Then came Lynch's calmly voiced lines that would raise the curtain on the next scene. Two very short sentences. Just three words.

"The dungeon." He pointed out the door. "Now."

Cat hurried to obey. Peanut and Gringo sensing her anxiety, followed closely behind. At the door to the Burgundy Rose, she firmly ordered them to stay outside.

Once inside, Lynch looked around. "I have to admit this place is perfect. Good work. When word of mouth gets out about this luxury dungeon, we'll be able to charge exorbitant rates."

Face tilted downward, Cat waited quietly just inside the door. With her entire future contingent on gaining a concession from him, she would do the job of sub perfectly tonight. Demure. Dutiful. Docile. At his service, even if the very thought made her nauseous.

"Do you like my gift?" His hand ran down the elegant, brushed-steel frame of the bed.

"Yes, Sir. It was a lovely surprise. Thank you, Sir."

He touched the burgundy satin duvet. "You've made your bed, I see. Now you'll get to lie in it. Chained, of course." Lynch chortled at his joke.

When his gaze speared her, she twittered appropriately. "Funny, Sir" she choked out.

"That'll be later," he added, moving to sit on the throne. He reclined on the brand new, red leather wingback chair. "Come here and strip."

Now that it was time, Cat found it harder to comply than she'd anticipated. She felt weak in the knees, but not in the good way she liked. Her heart pounded and all that wine she'd drunk had clearly been a mistake because it threatened to gag her. "Okay. Alright," she mumbled, pushing herself to take a step toward him.

"Okay?" he repeated, incredulously.

"I mean, Yes, Sir." Cat stumbled forward until she was right below him. *This shouldn't be hard.* She'd been naked before Master often for nearly three years. It was the kink pecking order—Lynch dressed and she undressed. Sometimes entire rooms of people in designer apparel or black leather—and she and the other subs, naked.

Staring down at her sundress, she started to unbutton it slowly.

"Look at me." Lynch wouldn't let her hide anything from him, not even her eyes. He watched closely, expecting to see the adoring regard a sub gave her Dom.

She really tried to infuse her gaze with something pleasant, but she feared that her growing loathing was easy to read. His eyes narrowed and jaw clenched. He was displeased.

When the dress gaped open, she slipped it off her shoulders to puddle at her feet. Now Cat stood before him in a pale-blue satin bra and panties. White lace bows decorating the front of both made her look gift-wrapped. Lynch's continued scrutiny made her skin crawl.

"I've treated you well, haven't I? Loaning you the money when no bank would. Buying you that special bed. And so much more over the years."

"Yes, Sir. I'm very grateful."

Where was this going, she questioned silently.

"That's a very pretty set, although you know I prefer your lingerie more Penthouse than Sunnybrook Farm." He indicated with his hand that she continue, and Cat reached behind to undo the clasp on her bra.

"You're still my submissive. By being here tonight you are confirming that."

Cat swallowed hard. Only one answer was acceptable if she hoped to keep her B&B. "Yes. Sir." She could barely force the words out but now it was done. She dropped her head in defeat.

"Eyes."

Her face jerked up. Then fear punched straight to her gut. Lynch wasn't just angry. He was enraged. His hands gripped the chair like claws and his eyes stabbed her. She'd never seen him like this before.

"So! As you've just reconfirmed. You are my sub. *Mine.* You belong to me and you will remain mine for as long as I want you. Given that, future goddess of domestic bliss, explain to me why you would go out on a date with the hired help?" He lurched to his feet, his voice roaring through the quiet space. "You let that nothing kiss you!"

"I…" Cat froze. An icy claw skittered down her spine. "I'm sorry," she wailed, dropping to her knees in supplication. "It was nothing. Just dinner. You know…to celebrate the work being done."

Lynch sat down, still so angry that he was near panting with fury. "You are not to go out with anyone else, kiss anyone else, not unless I order you to. Now get those panties off, unless you want me to whip you so hard they fall off in tatters."

"Yes, Sir," she squeaked, jumping to her feet and jerking her underpants down.

"You're very beautiful. Unique. An innocent and a sex-slut mixed into one gorgeous package." Lynch sighed as if the burden of wanting her was too much. She stood perfectly still, letting him stare at her body, dreading that he'd soon want to touch her too.

"Here." Lynch tossed her the rhinestone leather collar. Cat understood that he'd not accept any half-measures in her looks or actions here. She must go full subby or give up.

"You understand don't you, Bastet? I need to have you around me all the time, *always* naked. It's the only way I'll get you out of my system." Lynch seemed lost in thought. Babbling uncharacteristically. "The only thing that makes it bearable at the moment is knowing that very soon, you'll come to me. Then I can finally get my fill of you."

Lynch just sat there, barely moving, but the impact of his intense scrutiny was overwhelming. Claustrophobic. He was slowly devouring her, and when he spit her back out, she would become his version of herself. Small and helpless. The manic animosity and excitement in his expression was like a cloud of buzzing wasps ready to swarm over her. For the first time, Cat felt real fear in his presence. Only her love of this place and her desires for her future kept her from bolting.

"Sir?" Cat whispered. She had to be careful. "I still have a month before the payment. And maybe, together, we can find a way to make it work."

"We'll see."

His response gave her courage. Cat removed the gold choker and stepped forward, offering it up to him, with her face tilted down. Then she put on the debasing dog collar. She knelt down before him into his favorite presentation pose. Sitting on her heels, thighs spread wide to expose her pussy and hands behind her lower back. She even managed a somewhat adoring gaze. "Thank you, Sir."

"You're mine!"

Cat didn't argue. Too much was at stake.

"But your submission isn't enough," he railed. "I won't accept anything less than your total surrender. When you come to me in just a few weeks…and I know that you will…I want all of you. Freely given. Your body and your heart. I'll accept nothing less."

Cat couldn't answer. The truth, that she would never be able to give him that, would enrage him. Lynch waited for her confirmation. She bent down and stretched her arms forward, prostrating herself before him on the floor, letting her body do the lying for her.

He groaned. "God! I want to fuck you so hard. Pound you so hard. Take you the way we both love it. However, that won't happen tonight, sorry to disappoint. I can't bring myself to just use you like I can with the other girls. I *need* to hear your screams of ecstasy. But I won't give you that pleasure, not until you come to me ready to take your place in my home."

Cat was shocked, could hardly believe it. He thought it punishment, but instead it was a stunning reprieve. Her breasts still pressed to the cold slate floor, she tried to not let the relief show in her body.

"Once we're done tonight, I'm leaving. Knowing that I'll find our time together extremely arousing, I brought along my newest girl. She waits for me eagerly in a hotel suite in San Francisco. But you, my naughty pussy, won't get any relief. I'll leave you restrained on that fancy bed till morning, before I call and tell your friends to release you. Now before we get started, tell me how sorry you are for your behavior."

He had sounded casual. Like they were discussing dinner plans, and Cat began to wonder if Lynch was losing his sanity. Then she realized that once he left she'd lose the chance to negotiate. Cat didn't know what to do except try to mollify him by acting penitent.

"Sir," she called, forehead still resting on the floor. "I'm very sorry that I went out to dinner without your permission. That I let a man kiss me without your permission." It was a lie, given that she'd kissed him right back. She silently apologized to Mason. "I won't do it again, I promise, not as long as I'm your submissive."

"Let's get started." His suddenly gleeful tones sent shivers down her spine. "You may rise and get on the spanking bench."

Cat hesitated. What if she just refused? She still had a month, maybe she could find he money elsewhere.

"Get…up…now and take your punishment. You've admitted your mistake, so be a big girl."

She still couldn't bring herself to move.

"If you don't show contrition by accepting your discipline, I promise you I'll call my lawyers and start the process of ruining your B&B the very minute you fall short of your full payment. And if you safe-word to get out of it, I'll assume you're not really sorry and I'll call my lawyers. Do you understand me?"

"Yes, Sir." Woodenly, Cat pushed herself up off the floor and followed his instructions. Laying belly down on the tilted leather bench, she placed her legs on kneelers and her forearms on the armrests. She heard him move to the toys artfully arranged on the wall but didn't look.

"I'm not going to restrain you. No one will be able to say this was against your will, but hold on tight, Pussy mine, because every time you rise up before I say we're done will get you an extra stroke. Tell me that you understand and that you agree to be punished?"

"Yes, Sir. I understand and agree to be punished."

Cat heard him approaching and couldn't stop herself from looking over her shoulder to see what he would use. Lynch held a long, thin, bamboo cane, and when he saw her cringe, he smirked. He swiped it through the air a few times, the whistling demonstrating that even the air felt the sting. Cat turned rapidly away and lay her face down on the headrest.

Lynch trailed his hand slowly down along her skin, followed by the tip of the cane. Leaning over, he whispered like a ghost in her ear. "I could almost have overlooked you having dinner with a man not of my choosing, forgiven you for not asking for permission to go out with him, but your body and your lips are mine to control. That I cannot overlook or forgive."

Cat gasped at the vehemence in his quiet, angry voice.

She felt the slightest whoosh of air before the first strike hit her, a burning slash across the middle of her buttocks. The urge to flee nearly overwhelmed her, but she held tight to the bench.

Cat opened her mouth to beg him to tie her down but knew it was useless.

Whoosh. She shrieked as fire sliced again across the backs of her thighs.

Lynch strolled in a circle around her, keeping her in suspense, never indicating when or where it next would land.

Whoosh. She screamed. She shuddered.

The pain engulfed her like a firestorm. Gripping the table with fearsome strength, Cat let her mind drift on the swirling maelstrom. It wasn't subspace—the endorphin-filled state of pleasure-pain. But somewhere else Cat had learned to go to when she allowed Lynch the control over her she no longer wanted. Her mind shut down and she floated away, almost but not quite oblivious to the next violent streak of fire across her tortured ass.

Chapter 8

~ down the kinky rabbit hole

Mason never particularly liked Monday mornings, but this one was interminable. He just couldn't get the strange scene at the wine bar out of his head. Not the way that man Lynch had staked his claim on Cat. The guy didn't seem like any sort-of exboyfriend at all, when he'd possessively thrown his arm around her. Nor could Mason forget her panicked expression when he started to mention their date. And the doggie collars around two of her friends.

What the hell was that!

He'd thought about it all Sunday too, but today working next door to Sippity Doo Dah at the town's flower shop, it was all Mason could do not to go to her and demand an explanation. The recollections circled in his brain like a whirlpool of weird. It wasn't like he'd never heard of BDSM before. He didn't live in a cave. But out and about like that for anyone to see? And the way that Lynch guy acted like he literally owned Cat. Ordering her to sit. She'd worn a pretty piece of jewelry around her neck, but the similarity to her friends' collars was obvious. Or was it just a necklace? And why did he call her that strange name? And why had Cat addressed him as Mr. Steele?

What the hell was all that!

By the time he was heading home for lunch, his head ached. He had to put it out of his mind, catalog it as none of his business. But instead he found himself driving straight to Cat to get an explanation. Within minutes, he was turning onto her lane and searching for an excuse for his visit.

This is stupid! Mason put the transmission in reverse.

However, there was no backing out quietly with Peanut and Gringo already jumping around and barking like crazy. And then there was Cat. Pretty as sunshine on a bright spring day. Or a fall day. Or any ol' day, Mason realized, his gut seizing with forbidden yearning.

She stood stiffly on the porch. The casual flowered dress floated about her in the breeze, seeming too thin and short for this cool autumn weather.

"Hey," he called, pitching a casually friendly tone as he climbed from his truck. "I, um, just thought I'd run one more test of the pipes, so I'm doubly sure nothing can go wrong when the inspector finally comes."

"Ah. Okay."

"Great."

Mason headed around back to the pump house on his fictional quest. Then he spent the next fifteen minutes turning knobs and running water through pipes for no reason at all. Cat was cleaning the house after her friends' weekend visit. Neither mentioned the confrontation at Sippity Doo Dah.

As he went through the farmhouse pretending to check everything, Mason was hyper-aware of her presence, and something was off. He had first thought her stiff stance when he'd arrived was due to irritation with him, but Cat also moved strangely. Woodenly.

When he saw her wince as she picked up a basket of dirty sheets, he hurried to her side. "Here, let me carry that." Cat seemed reluctant to hand it over.

They walked together to her laundry facilities in the small freestanding garage. "Are you okay?" he asked.

"Sure," Cat replied, but the smile she gave him was brittle, a forced parting of the lips that looked as painful as the way she walked. "Just put it there, and thanks." She pointed to a table near the washing machine.

"I'll just get back to it then," he said. Within minutes he'd finished flushing every toilet and trying every spigot in the farmhouse and had nothing left to fake. He still didn't know what he wanted to say to her or what to ask about the other night.

Deciding it was a useless mission, he headed back downstairs and heard her groan, the jarring sound of someone in pain. And then he heard it again. He followed the groans to the open door of the master suite. Cat bent down awkwardly to retrieve another clean pillowcase from the basket on the floor, and he got a quick glimpse of bright red welts across the back of her thighs and purplish discoloration, like skin beginning to bruise. His stomach curdled at the sight of her injuries with the potency of heavyweight punch to the gut.

"What the hell!" he thundered, stepping toward her. "What happened to you?"

Cat jerked around to see Mason in the doorway. Her face blanching, she hurled a denial forcefully, but her voice cracked at the end. "Nothing. What do you mean?"

Stepping closer, he could see her eyes were bright with unshed tears. She backed up a step.

He wanted to grab her. Shake her. Yell at her for allowing this to happen. He wanted to slam his fist into the wall—or into someone's face. And he could guess whose. Most of all, he wanted to see how badly she was hurt and then take care of her. Pull her into his arms and protect her.

To stop himself from rushing her, Mason stood rigidly stiff, his knees locked and his fists clenched. However, he couldn't make his voice normal—the tinge of panic and ton of outrage came out with the low-pitched intensity of a wolf's growl. "I saw welts across the back of your thighs, and I think there are more."

She forced a laugh. "Really. It's nothing."

The understanding, gentlemanly version of Mason was pretty much gone by then. Replaced by alpha-male army soldier, an attitude that had gotten him through two Iraqi tours. Once turned on, military Mason never took no for an answer, kept powering forward until he achieved his mission. "If that's so, then how about you sit…there." He pointed at a wooden bench under the window.

"You're being silly."

Mason remembered the way she reacted to a strong tone. He weighted his voice with command and mimicked a sergeant in basic training. "Sit down. Now!"

"This is absurd. Really absurd." But she was already moving toward the window seat.

Mason folded his arms and spread his feet slightly. And waited.

Cat threw a 'see-I'm-fine' grin his way as she lowered herself gingerly to the bench. However, she winced when her ass touched the hard wood. A brief groan escaped her lips.

"There. See. I'm fine." She smiled up at him, but it was really more of a grimace.

"Cat!" Mason's haunted cry was as filled with agony as her forced smile. He rushed to her and lifted her to standing. "I'm sorry. I didn't mean to cause you pain."

"You didn't cause it. I did."

"What do you mean? Those welts couldn't be accidental. They looked like…like someone had whipped your legs. Like…"

Sudden clarity made him gasp, his hands tightening on her arms.

The collars. Her odd behavior. The Burgundy Rose.

An art studio that wasn't an art studio.

The shock of it made his head swim. Sweat broke out on his brow. Mason almost did shake her then.

He forced himself to let go and stepped away, backing across the room. "You…Let…Him…Beat…You." It wasn't a question, but still he wanted to hear her confirm it. "Tell me it's not true?"

Cat wouldn't meet his gaze. "Mason, it's not what you think. I'm a—"

"Like hell it isn't. That guy Lynch beat you and I'm calling the police."

"No! You can't." She rushed forward in jerky, wooden movements to grab his arms.

"Give me one good reason not to."

"Because…" Cat seemed afraid, as if whatever she had to say would be worse than what he'd already learned. She took a deep breath and looked him in the eye. "Because he's my Dom and I *gave* him permission."

Mason staggered back. It was true then. He'd guessed it, accused her of it, but still hoped he was wrong. He scrubbed his fingers through his hair. Sucked in harsh breaths. It hurt in his chest to think of anyone hurting her, causing her pain. "I don't understand." He managed to push the words out, but it felt like he was chewing sandpaper.

She turned away from him, seeming unwilling to meet his eyes, and shuffled over to the window to look out into the yard. Seeing the Burgundy Rose in the distance she said, "Come with me. I want to show you something."

Mason followed her to the old stone shed. Neither spoke, and even the dogs were quiet as they trailed the silent couple. She punched in the lock code and shoved the door open.

He walked boldly inside to the center. His eyes bulged. Mason had already guessed it would be like something out of that movie *Fifty Shades*, but the impact of all that menacing furniture and creepy implements hanging on the wall stunned him. It was a torture chamber that would make the Marquis de Sade leer with pleasure.

He rounded on her. "This isn't an art studio."

She laughed then, his sunshine girl happy for a moment. "Nope."

Cat shuffled toward him. "I don't expect you to understand and would never have told you. But I'm pleased in a way, because now you understand why we can't date. It has nothing to do with you. I'm a sexual submissive. So we're not compatible. It doesn't matter how much I like you. I know myself, and sooner or later I'll grow bored because vanilla sex isn't enough for me."

Mason felt like he'd fallen down the rabbit hole but into an alternate universe where the Mad Hatter carried a flogger and the Queen of Hearts was a dominatrix. And Alice, all sunshine and sweetness, liked to have her ass whipped till she couldn't sit down. Or until she climaxed.

He pushed his fingers through his hair again. "So, you're saying that Lynch did this to you so you could...orgasm? That you can't do that without it."

"Not exactly. At least not to that extent." She grinned crookedly at him. "That..." She gestured in the general vicinity of her behind. "That was punishment for my misbehavior."

"What!" Mason bellowed, feeling like he really had landed in Wonderland, the creepy Timothy Burton kind that would give him nightmares. "I'm gonna kill him." He turned toward the door.

"Mason. Stop!" Cat yelled just as loudly. "You've no right to interfere. It's my business, *my* life. And whether you or I like it, he's still my Master."

"Your *Master?* Like he owns you. Like a slave?" The idea made him nauseous.

"It's an arrangement we have. I haven't yet been released from my contract with him."

"That can't be legal. But, whatever." Mason started toward the door again. "My fist in that bastard's face will release you. Trust me."

"He's gone."

That made him slow down. Pause long enough to play through everything she'd said. Leaning his forehead against the door, Mason took deep calming breaths. "Back to L.A.?"

"Yes."

Mason straightened and turned to face her. "Is he coming back?"

"I hope not. He's not invited."

"But you still want him? Not me."

She sighed, the sound loud in the silent space. "No, actually, I don't. I haven't really wanted him to be my Dom for a while now."

Hope rose swiftly. Mason lurched toward her.

"But I still want a dominant for my lover. It's who I am. What I need." She stepped right up to him, so close he could smell her fresh flowery scent. "You're a nice guy who deserves a nice, normal girl. I wish you nothing but happiness in your life, and I'm really grateful for your hard work on my remodel."

She's showing me the door, and all because I won't hit her?

"I just don't get it." Anger fueled his stance with aggression and his tone with virulence. "Do you mean to tell me that if I beat your ass, you'll let me fuck you? Is that it? Well give me a damn bat cause I'm all game."

"I think you should leave now."

He searched her eyes but all he saw was firm determination and, perhaps, a little sadness.

Cat repeated, "I need you to leave now."

So he left. Never once looking back as he walked to his truck. He'd been wrong about her. All that springtime innocence was an illusion that hid something dark and dirty. He understood that now.

And, anyway. *She* didn't want him.

Chapter 9

~ time slows down, then speeds up

Mason had not talked with Cat in three days. Actually, 71 hours, 32 minutes, and 5 seconds.

It seemed like forever since he'd held her and kissed her on their date.

It seemed like just a millisecond ago that he'd discovered she'd been beaten by a sadist or a madman. He wasn't sure which or if they were the same thing. His fury was a raging storm, making his blood rush and his hands fist. He still needed to punch something.

And in this strange purgatory of yearning and fury, Mason was confused by contradictory desires. He didn't understand how this beautiful, intelligent woman could get off on serving a man as a sex slave. But worse, why did the thought of Cat on her knees serving him make his dick hard? It made him *want* to dominate her. Not hurt her. *Never that.* But treat her in a way that went against everything he believed about respecting women, about treating them as equals, about making a happy marriage.

His dad had once told him that a good marriage could be had for the price of two words: "Yes, Dear." It had been a joke, of course, that the husband should always agree with his wife, but he'd seen the easy give and take in his parents' relationship.

Though Mason had never thought about it, he assumed it was as true in his parents' bedroom as anywhere else in their shared life.

But now Mason hungered, like a man starving, to go back to that outrageous place, the Burgundy Rose. And feed the hunger with Cat. He wasn't sure if she would let him near her after the way he'd behaved, or whether he should pursue it given his conflicted feelings. Regardless, Mason *needed* to talk with her, and now he had an excuse to contact her. He had made it happen, his good news.

He held his cell to his ear and listened to the rings, hoping she'd answer. Relief sighed through him when she did.

"Hello, Mason." Her voice was subdued, cautious.

"Hi, Cat."

I've missed you. I'm sorry. Please let me back in your life.

Instead, he said, "I've got two things to tell you. One is good news."

"Oh." It sounded flat. Noncommittal.

"I was able to pull in some—"

"What are you doing here?" Her tone suddenly pitched higher.

He didn't understand. "Cat, I'll leave you alone if you don't—"

"You have no right," she yelled, cutting him off. "I've got another two weeks."

Mason realized she wasn't talking to him when he heard a man's voice, but the words were unintelligible over her dogs' wild barking.

"Cat! Cat!" Mason shouted into his cell. Fear seized him. Someone was there in her home. Someone who hadn't been invited, who wasn't welcome. His heart pounded painfully inside the near-choking confines of his constricted chest.

There was another heated volley between her and the man, the barking cacophony overriding it, but the sound was also muted, like she held the phone to her chest.

Then she was back. "Mason, I've got to go."

"No wait. Who's there? Are you—"

She hung up on him.

Shit. Shit. Shit.

Mason paced the room. He wanted to go to her, but Cat had already told him not to interfere in her life. That she didn't want to see him again. But she was in trouble, and he was pretty damn sure he knew who was there.

Mason grabbed his car keys and bolted from his house. Within seconds, he was gunning his truck down Main Street. His eyes flicked to the time on the dashboard. He'd be there in less than five. He hoped it was fast enough.

He turned onto Pope Street. Only a few blocks to go, but it seemed endless. Seeing her driveway, barely slowing, Mason yanked the wheel to the right and careened up the lane. Racing forward the last hundred feet, he slammed on the brakes at the last second.

An unfamiliar Mercedes sedan sat next to Cat's SUV. Mason ran passed it and leapt straight over the stairs onto the porch. The sound of angry voices carried through the window. Her dogs turned toward him but this time they didn't block him, parting so he could pass. He yanked open the door and rushed into the kitchen, the dogs slipping in with him.

Mason's military training kicked in, and he instantly took in the situation. Cat and Lynch faced each other on opposite sides of the table. Heated emotion filled the kitchen like thick dark smoke. Radiating menace, Lynch pointed at the slave collar on the table. "Put it on." Cat was shaking her head, her hands up as if to ward him off. Rage filled Mason at finding the sadistic bastard anywhere near her.

His abrupt entrance drew their attention, disbelief flashing across their faces. Quick as a gunshot, their expressions morphed. Lynch's to hatred. Cat's to… It took Mason an extra second to recognize what he saw on her face, but then he knew. Hope.

It freed him to act on her behalf. "What the hell are you doing here, Lynch?"

He ignored Mason, directing his attention to Cat. "Naughty Pussy, I told you not to allow curs in the house."

"It's my house."

Lynch continued as if she hadn't spoken. "I want that collar around your neck. Now. It will show the hired help who owns you and remind you of what you really are. A pain-slut who craves the red-hot imprint of her master's hand."

Mason stalked to Lynch. "Get the hell out of here." Again, his military background came into play. He stood tall, determined, and unwavering.

Slowly, as if Lynch could hardly believe the other man's audacity, he turned his arrogant glare on Mason. "This doesn't concern you. Pussy and I have an understanding." The man's timbre turned condescending. "*My* slave has needs you couldn't possibly satisfy. You wouldn't know what to do with such a prize. Nor how to tame it, which, evidently, is a job I haven't yet finished." Lynch started around the table toward Cat.

Hands fisted, Mason moved closer still, his stance at the ready. "You fucking asshole."

"Mason! What are you doing here?" She moved around the table toward him.

Cat's cry stopped him. He scowled at Lynch, daring him to take one step closer to her.

Not taking his eyes off the man, he replied, "I know that I have no place in your life, but I won't let that asshole hurt you again. Not ever."

He stepped forward to block Lynch. Nose-to-nose, eyes narrowed on his enemy and Cat safely behind him, Mason could almost breath again.

Lynch shocked him by laughing. A deep, amused chortle followed by a patronizing smirk, as if Mason were the stupidest man on the planet. "You really don't get it, do you?" Lynch tilted his head in Cat's direction. "*It* wants to be dominated. *It* needs debasement and pain. You would bore it to tears, frustrated and horny. So, little vanilla boy, go home and play with children your own age."

"Not a fucking chance. And stop calling her, it!" Mason yelled.

As if finally realizing that Mason was a threat, Lynch altered his stance, suddenly exuding power and authority. The transformation was as real as if he'd donned a dark cloak of dominance. And Mason saw for the first time what the term 'Dom' really meant. The Master's supremacy was undeniable and strangely compelling, demanding deference.

Utilizing all his reserves of military might, Mason held fast, maintaining eye contact and readiness against his opponent.

The Master looked unperturbed. He didn't attempt to step around Mason, speaking through him to Cat as if he wasn't there. "Pussy, I'm finding this thoroughly tiresome. You know full well what's going to happen. Without the inspection, you're going to miss your first payment. Then, to save your beloved aunt's farmhouse, you'll willingly serve your time as my house slave. The sooner you start, the sooner I'll be done with you."

Lynch tilted his head and flicked an elegant finger in the direction of the door. "And tell the hired help to get out, because this distasteful business has made my palms itch to spend some quality time with you. So, put on the damn collar and get your ass to the dungeon."

"Fuck you," snarled Mason. He pulled back his fist.

Cat leapt forward and grabbed his raised arm. "It's okay. It's my mess, not yours. I made it and I'll deal with the consequences."

"Cat! You can't choose this. I won't let you." Even if she refused to ever speak to him again, Mason would not let her sacrifice herself.

Lynch nodded approvingly at her, a gloating smile curling his mouth. "You're forgiven, Pussy mine. Now that you're making the right choice."

Mason's hands clenched, but she stepped between the two men. "Master Lynch, I truly appreciate everything you've done for me over the years, but we're through." Her tone was resolute and brave. "I will not go back to Malibu with you, and I will never, *ever,* become your live-in."

"What?" Disbelief whipped the pomposity from Lynch's expression.

"It's not going to happen. Now I want you to leave my house."

"How dare you! I lent you seventy-two thousand dollars for this place. You can't kick me out."

"This is still my house. At least, for another five weeks, so get out."

Good for you. Mason wanted to clap and cheer. Instead, he put his hand on her shoulder and squeezed reassuringly. She placed her small one over his, and gladness welled within him.

Lynch looked surprised by her command of the situation. "My kitten has claws." He chuckled, his mirth clearly false.

Then he noticed the two of them touching and anger returned, his eyes narrowing on her. "Once you grasp what you've done, you'll come crawling. I'm sure of it. But you'll pay for your disrespect with a pound of flesh, pay till you're red and raw. And I'll keep training you until you finally understand your purpose…until the only thing that matters to you is pleasing me."

Rage overtook Mason and he pulled free of her, ready to blast his fist into Lynch's evil face.

But Cat surprised Mason again. She didn't cower under the Dom's crazy onslaught. Somehow, she seemed to grow taller, stand prouder, and in a fine, strong voice, repeated, "Even if I lose everything, *absolutely* everything, I will never again be yours. Never. *Now get the hell out before I call the police!*"

Lynch looked like he wanted to argue but, surprising them, just shrugged. "Your mistake." He walked out of the kitchen without another word.

Mason's admiration for Cat went supernova, like his heart would burst. She'd made the right choice for her future, regardless of the cost, and he hoped there might be a small place in her life for him too. He reached out and squeezed her hand, while he remaining vigilant, listening for the sound of Lynch's car disappearing down the road.

He turned to Cat, ready to apologize for interfering without any right, but she launched herself into his arms. Mason accepted this gift and held her tightly. Whispering endearments. Telling her how proud he was. Never wanting to let her go.

After a moment, they heard the unmistakable sound of a car approaching and froze. Hands fisted again, Mason turned toward the door. The dogs started barking too, ready to do their part to protect her.

"I'll handle this," Mason said, gently moving her behind him, but Cat resisted.

Taking his hand, she said, "We'll handle this." Together, they walked to the porch.

But it wasn't the same car, and then they could see who was in it. She turned to him excitedly. "It's the inspector. He's here!"

Bart Peterson parked and got out. "Hi, is it okay if I do the inspection now?"

"Yes, of course," Cat replied eagerly. "But I thought there wasn't a single opening in weeks?"

Peterson scratched his head, looking thoughtful. "That's true, but someone important must have pulled some strings at the mayor's office, because this order got moved to the top of the priority list. Now if it's okay with you, I'll get started, 'cause I've got a bunch more to do today."

"Sure. Go right ahead."

Cat turned to Mason, her eyes sparkling. "Did you know about this?"

He nodded. "I called in a bunch of favors and that was one of the reasons that I called you earlier."

They followed the inspector around, holding hands, and within a short time Cat had the approval she needed and could open for business within the week. She thanked the inspector and, after waving goodbye from the porch, reached up to kiss Mason on the cheek.

"Thank you so much. I don't know how I can repay you."

"You can start by giving me another kiss," he joked.

And she did.

Throwing herself back into his arms, Cat planted a big one on his lips. Mason grabbed the chance to hold her, pulling her close and deepening the kiss. Her hands crept into his hair, and he slid his hands around her back, enjoying the feel of her pressed against him. He put everything into the kiss, stroking her tongue with his, caressing her back, and sliding one leg between her thighs to press against her there. When they finally pulled apart, she was breathless and he was rock hard.

Was Cat aroused too?

After everything he'd heard about her sexual needs, he couldn't be sure. How do you ask a woman if she's aroused?

But Cat spoke first. "You said you had two things to tell me when you called earlier."

Mason wanted to do it right. He took her hand and led her to the porch swing. After they sat, he took both her hands in his. "The other thing has several parts. First, I want to apologize for my reaction the other day when I found out about your lifestyle. It was a shock, but I behaved badly. I'm sorry."

"That's okay. I hadn't planned to tell you because, well, it's a shock to everyone. My sibs and most definitely my parents don't know either."

"The next thing I want to say is that I've spent the last three days reading up on BDSM and thinking about us. I want you to know that I don't judge you. To be absolutely truthful, some of it sounds smokin' hot. I've even dreamed about you tied to a bed, that bed." Mason pointed in the direction of the Burgundy Rose. "It's a fantasy I can't get out of my head."

"Are you saying you want to try it?" Mason liked the eagerness in her eyes but didn't want to disappoint her later.

"I think so. Maybe. I definitely want to learn more about it. But, Cat," he trailed a finger gently down her cheek, "I can't imagine ever wanting to strike you and it seems like something you need."

"I see."

He wasn't sure what that meant, but he plunged ahead. "The last thing I wanted to say, to ask, was if you would go out with me again. We're great together, mostly, although maybe not in the bedroom, but I'd still like to get to know you better. What do you say, are you willing to give a *vanilla* a try? I mean we both gotta eat, right?"

Cat answered him in an unexpected way. She threw her arms around him and kissed him, thoroughly, aggressively, the swing rocking with her enthusiasm. Mason was more than willing to let her take the lead. When she pulled back they were both panting, and he had to cross his arms over his legs, hiding the huge bulge in his pants.

"Was that your way of accepting my invitation to dinner?"

Cat didn't say a word as she rose to look down at him. She extended her hand and he took it. Mason let her lead him from the swing but wasn't sure what he'd do if she took him to the Burgundy Rose, her Marquis de Pain palace.

She didn't, leading him instead to the farmhouse's master suite.

"Are you sure?" he asked quietly.

Cat didn't immediately answer. Gazing into his eyes, she seemed to be giving his question serious thought.

Please. Please. Please, he begged silently.

He was holding on by a thread so badly did he want her to say yes.

She stepped closer and whispered, "Yes. But I…" Anxiety on her face, she looked at the waiting king-size bed. He was rattled, wondering if it was too boring for her. For him, it would be nirvana as long as she would let him worship her body on it.

"What is it? If it's too soon, let's not." It was his gift to her, the size of which Cat would never know. With effort, he turned his back on the bed and on his rampaging physical need.

"I'm not sure what's normal anymore." She sounded lost. "It's been a long time since I've had normal sex. You know, sex where I wasn't told exactly what to do and how to do it. I don't want to be a bore but, maybe, if I'm not doing something or doing the wrong thing…" She trailed off, and bit her lip.

Mason tried very hard to match her serious expression. He wanted to shout with joy, laugh like an idiot, and dance around the room.

Instead he quietly clarified, "Are you asking me to guide you? Tell you what I want?"

"Yes," she said eagerly. "If you want, I mean."

Then Mason did laugh, boisterously, sweeping Cat up and twirling her around. "Oh, honey! If that's your only worry, don't give it another thought. I'd have to be a fuckin' idiot if I didn't like the sound of you asking me to tell you what feels good in bed."

"Oh," she gasped, before joining in his glee.

Mason kissed her on the lips and set her down. And just to be sure she didn't have any remaining doubts on the subject, he reiterated, "Cat, it would be my great pleasure, like super super great, to instruct you on the sexy things that rock my boat. There's nothing I'd like more. Seriously."

Cat looked pleased, if also somewhat surprised. Mason tried to rein in his over-the-top excitement.

"Thank you, Sir." She looked stricken. "I mean, thank you, Mason."

"Honey, *darling*, you can call me anything you want…just don't call me late for fuckin' you!"

He hugged her tight. "And Cat, the very first thing I'm going to ask of you is to promise me you'll do the same for me. I mean it. Tell me what things I'm doing you like and what else I can do, so I can please you as much as you please me. Deal?"

Cat laughed with delight, looking more carefree than he'd ever seen her. She held out her hand to shake, and when he'd taken it, she said, "Deal," pumping his hand vigorously.

There'd been enough talking, Mason decided. He pulled on her hand, drawing her closer, and then slid his hands around her body to drag her up against him. God, it felt good to have her back in his arms. When Cat remained passive, he begged, "Touch me. Put your arms around me. Explore my body. Do anything you fucking want, just keep your hands on me."

Cat giggled and immediately placed her hands on either side of his head. She dragged his face down to hers. Mason happily went with that and smashed his mouth down on hers. For endless moments, he explored the delicious sensations. His tongue slipping in to tangle with hers. Nearly out of his mind with wanting her, he cupped her tight ass and ground his erection against her.

She moaned and matched his movements with her pelvis. He was thrilled that Cat had taken his request to heart. Her hands moved about his body as if she wanted to feel every single part of him at once, and everywhere she roamed—biceps, back, pectorals—his skin flared with heat.

Mason groaned into her mouth, thinking he would go insane if he didn't get her naked so they could be skin to skin, but she was one step ahead of him, tugging on the buttons of his shirt. Laughing, he pulled away to yank the shirt over his head, and Cat followed his example, tearing off her sundress. In between each article of clothing that flew, they flung themselves back at each other, mouths meeting hungrily, hands frantically groping, wanting to touch each other everywhere. Mason reveled in the feel of her bare skin pressed against his, but when they finally pulled back so he could remove his briefs he stopped dead at the sight of Cat dropping her bra to the floor.

She stood there before him, panting and proud. Her blond hair hung about her shoulders like a veil of spun gold. Her sparkling sapphire eyes called to him with passionate desire. But it was her pale breasts and their pert rose centers that made him want to fall to his knees before her.

"Catriona" he breathed, his voice heavy with lust. "You're the most beautiful thing I've ever seen."

"I need you," she whispered. Cat stepped forward and her delicate fingers grasped his briefs and tugged them down. Before he even realized what she planned, she was on her knees and her pretty pink lips were slipping around the end of his dick.

"Cat. You don't need…I don't expect…"

He wanted to tell her that it wasn't necessary. That she didn't have to serve him. That he wanted to serve her. But it was too late. He was too far gone. Once she buried his dick in her hot mouth, he lost the ability to talk or think or do anything…except feel the pleasure. Feel the way her lips formed a tight ring of suction around his cock. Feel the wet velvety heat as she drew him deep inside her mouth, her face pressed to his groin. Feel her tongue lave him mercilessly till he could barely stand upright.

Her hands grasped his butt, using him for leverage, and he shuddered at the erotic feel of her fingers squeezing and kneading his ass. She pulled back and cool air washed over his heated dick wet with her saliva. Just at the point of no return, she swooped forward again, sucking him even deeper. Cat repeated this over and over, pumping him until he started to shudder with the need to explode in her mouth. His hands found her head, and had Mason any control at all he would have pushed Cat free so he could worship her, but he had none. He was reduced to a thing of pure sensation, his entire world nothing but the feel of her mouth servicing his aching cock.

Somehow he found his voice. "Please Cat," he cried. "I want to fuck your pussy, give you pleasure too. I can't hold back."

Not quite releasing him, Cat stated, "This is what *I* want."

Then she started again. Fellating him relentlessly, Cat wouldn't let up, wouldn't stop, until Mason was unable to resist meeting her with his own thrusts, until he was feverishly fucking her mouth. He drove faster and harder, until he juddered one last time. With an ecstatic roar, he exploded into her mouth.

But Cat still didn't stop, kept pumping until he was drained and couldn't take anymore.

Panting, he bent over, hands to knees, trying to catch his breath. Finding her mouth near, Mason claimed it. Using his hands to lock her face to his, his tongue continued to feverishly fuck her mouth. He could taste what must be him mixed with her uniqueness, and he could feel her strong tongue twirling with his.

Barely aware of his actions, Mason pulled her upright and scooped her into his arms. He carried her to the giant bed and stretched her out on it so that he could begin a journey of exploration across her peaks and valleys, teasing and nipping and licking. He was rewarded by her responsiveness. Her whimpers were like an erotic melody, her pleas like sonnets, and her shudders a delicate dance. She was a masterpiece, and Mason couldn't stop meticulously playing every inch of her, not until he'd learned what made her sing and drew from Cat her total surrender.

"Please, Mason," she begged. "I want you."

"Shh," he murmured. He'd grown hard again so rapidly it took him by surprise, but he wanted to see how much he could push her. "I'm so far from done with you, it's like we haven't even started."

"Mason!" she cried, but her needy hunger was music to him. She reached for him, trying to bring his pelvis to her pussy.

He leaned over her, studying the magnificent mounds of her breasts, fascinated by their perfect pink peaks. Cat almost frantically pulled at him, trying to drag at least a hand to the part of her that ached the most. Without breaking his meditative contemplation of her nipples, he found her arms and dragged them above her head. Holding her wrists against the pillow with one hand, it left the other free to explore. He gave one mound a gentle squeeze. His finger flicked the nipple, and Cat involuntarily arched into him. Bending closer, he slowly brought his mouth to her breast. He dragged his wet tongue in a circle around one glorious tight bud, loving the sound of her eager moans.

Then, in the same way that Cat had pulled his cock into her wet depths, he sucked her teat into his hungry mouth. Acting as if he had all the time in the world, he played and tugged on that one glorious tit as she writhed beneath him. He could spend hours worshiping her breasts.

Mason moved to its twin, his eyes studying the other peak with equal concentration.

"Mason!" she cried desperately. She squirmed and whimpered. "Please!"

"Shh." But he gave her some relief, his hand gliding down across her flat belly, through her damp blond curls, to tease her body just above the spot that he knew ached for him.

Begging for his hand, she spread her thighs wide and lifted her pelvis in welcome.

Mason sucked her untried peak into his mouth at the same time his thumb unerringly found the nub of her pleasure. He bit her nipple sharply and flicked her clit. Cat about came off the bed, crying out and writhing beneath him. He grinned around the breast in his mouth, loving that she wanted him as much as he wanted her. But he wasn't ready to let her come. While he continued to feast on her breast, his fingers grazed her inner thighs, teased her wet folds, and slipped inside her hole. Cat bucked her encouragement. Mason continued to play her body mercilessly until she was thrashing about, eyes tightly shut, pulling uselessly to free her arms, and moaning incoherently.

Her wild abandon was beautiful, and suddenly she had all the power. Cat intoxicated him, drugging him into a mind-numbing state of urgent need. He could think of nothing else but sliding his throbbing shaft into her hole. Nothing else in the world mattered. Mason had become her slave.

"Cat!" he cried, rising to look at her.

He couldn't manage anything more. Her eyes popped open to meet his, and he silently begged her.

"Yes!" she murmured.

He released her wrists and started to cover her with his body. Then hesitated.

"The night stand," she said, rolling toward it. Yanking it open, she pulled out a condom and tossed it to Mason. "For my future guests, you know."

Within seconds, he had it open and on. Cat's hungry eyes on his dick made him harder.

He moved into position over her and, holding himself up, stared down into her deep blue eyes. His dick, nestled at the apex of her thighs, jerked with wanting. "Cat?"

She answered by tugging on his hips and spreading her thighs.

Mason slid home in one powerful thrust. He lowered his upper body so that he could kiss her and began thrusting in and out. She smiled against his lips and joined the dance, meeting each joining. They moved like one, plunging and bucking. Sensation washed over him, drowning him in pleasure. Her hot tongue rasping against his. Her tight pussy gripping his cock. Her breasts damp with sweat sliding against his chest. Delicious friction everywhere.

Mason was desperate for more. He drove into her over and over. Faster and faster. Cat matched him, head thrown back and eyes closed. She held on and frantically rubbed against him, offering little encouraging cries. Grunting and panting and moaning, they moved as one, always seeking more.

Mason was almost there, his groin tightening in a relentless drive to find oblivion, but he wanted her there with him. He grunted encouragement too until he couldn't.

Unable to hold back, pleasure exploded through Mason. He roared. "Oh, Cat!"

He made one last powerful thrust as waves and waves of ecstasy rolled through him, so powerful that he almost didn't hear her answering shudders. Delight that she was cresting with him, bucking wildly on his shaft, made the euphoria last for endless moments, until at last they grew still.

Breathing in deeply, her scent wafting through him, Mason slowly opened his eyes. He searched her expression, needing to know if it had been enough. Cat gave him the hugest smile ever. Her joy spread across her face and sparkled in her eyes.

Relief relaxed Mason. "Hi, beautiful." He smiled down at her.

"Man! You're one fine fuck," Cat responded, grinning. "When can we do that again?"

Mason laughed, loud and booming. "Soon, baby, soon. But I'm not superman. Gotta give Mr. Happy a minute to recover."

"Okay, but not too long...Sir." Tilting her head, she winked at him.

He'd been right all along. He was a goner. Cat owned him body and soul, and Mason was seized by a powerful longing to stay right where he was in this moment. Inside her. Forever.

He vowed to make Cat so happy that she, too, would never want to leave.

Chapter 10

~ fall color tour rush

During the past two months the new couple had worked together to make the B&B launch a huge success. Between his army buddies and wives coming for the fall color tour, the Tulip House was booked solid, while her kinky L.A. friends made sure the Burgundy Rose saw a lot of action, too. As a result Cat was able to make her first big payment to Lynch on time. Mason had already decided there was no way he was letting the sadist near Cat again, but it was certainly better all around if she were able to meet the schedule.

"So, did the check finally clear?" Mason tried for calm but he couldn't lose the steely edge of resentment. He covered it by gently rocking the swing where they sat drinking their preferred libations.

"Yes, sweet guy, it did." Cat leaned over and pecked him on the cheek. "You can stop worrying about me."

"I'll always worry when it comes to your safety and happiness." Mason put his bottle down on the side table and pulled her onto his lap, wineglass and all.

"Whoa!" Cat tried not to spill any wine as he hauled her onto his thighs. He loved the way she felt, her warm behind nestled on his crotch.

Giving him a mock glare, she admonished, "This is the expensive stuff."

He watched as her pink tongue slipped out to lick a drip of wine that trickled down the side of the glass. Nearly continuous hunger, like he'd never felt before in his life, poured back to his groin. He couldn't get enough of this woman. "Will you do that to me, if I dribble wine on my…" He'd meant it as a tease, but it came out hoarse with need and dark with desire.

He dropped his gaze to his crotch for a second before returning to meet her eyes. Hers flared with delight and with matching hunger.

Mason didn't wait for Cat's response, but took her mouth in a devouring, demanding kiss. His tongue thrusting inside, he could taste the expensive wine…and her. The sinfully sweet taste that was Cat's alone. He deepened the kiss, ready to haul her up and carry her caveman-like to her attic suite. He didn't give a wit, if any guests saw what they were about.

"Wait." Cat broke the kiss. "There's something I want to tell you and I think it's important, but I didn't want to say it in our—I mean—my bedroom."

Mason liked her slip. Liked thinking of the place as theirs. Not that he wanted any part of her business. Just that it thrilled him, more than it probably should, the idea of them sharing a home together, eventually maybe sharing a life together.

But there were unsettled issues between them, and he wondered if that was what Cat needed to discuss. He had never asked about the BDSM side of her life, and she hadn't brought it up in the nearly two months they'd been a couple. He avoided the Burgundy Rose, and perhaps she had noticed. It wasn't that he was appalled by her needs, initial shock aside, but rather he was appalled at himself. The wicked allure of the dungeon played out in his dreams, while his conscious mind was still angry about the abuse she'd endured. The bruises were long gone, but if she ever asked that he beat her like that, Mason knew he wouldn't be able to do it. It had taken a lot of soul searching and some research to even begin to understand her needs and his new feelings. He wasn't ready to discuss it.

Would this be the day Cat asked him to hit her and then what would he do? He could never hurt her, but he couldn't let her go either. She was too important to him now.

Some weekenders pulled into the driveway after their day of wine-tasting, and Cat slipped from his lap. Mason let her go and took a deep calming breath. He'd make it work, no matter what the issue. "What is it you want to tell me?"

She seemed to realize that he was tense, and gave him a little pat on the hand to go with the reassuring smile she sent his way. "It's good news. Really. Just not a topic I want brought into the place where we make love."

Mason felt some of the tension ease, while he watched her greeting the guests and welcoming them back after their day of sightseeing. After a few minutes the couple went inside.

"Okay. Shoot." Mason grabbed his bottle of Lucky Beagle Brew and downed a big gulp to give himself something to do, rather than wait for the ball to drop. Or, rather, the crop, or flogger, or whatever implement of torture she might ask him to use on her.

"It's about Master Lynch."

Mason's hand tightened on the bottle so forcefully he wondered why it didn't break in his hand. Speaking was impossible, so he just sat there.

"The good news is that Master Lynch has a new house slave. Sam called earlier to tell me. Completely out of the blue, he initiated Amber last night, branding her Teicu after the Aztec goddess of sexual appetite. Aphrodite's already packed and gone. Isn't that great."

Mason relaxed so suddenly, the tension whooshing out felt like a deflating balloon. He wanted to muster a matching excitement, but the elephant in the room waited by the porch stairs. Would it stampede through their budding relationship?

When he didn't speak, she added, "I was thinking we should really celebrate. Go to town and try out the new Vine & Dine Bistro. My treat." Her smile was back, breathtaking in its sunshiny freshness.

And just like that Mason bounced back. Cat made him feel like it was always springtime, like the tulips were blooming and life was new and hopeful.

"You bet. Let's celebrate, but no way am I letting you treat me. My momma would tan my hide if I did that, and I'm not joking." Mason grinned, to lessen the impact, but he would do everything in his power to make sure she never fell short on making repayments.

"Okay, but if you'd rather we could stay here. I know you've been going down to the city so much lately for all those business meetings…so I'd understand if you didn't feel like eating out."

Mason knew she was curious about his frequent visits to San Francisco, but it wasn't something he was ready to tell her about yet. He hoped that in the end it would please her, but for now he ignored the question in her tone. "Just so I understand, does that mean Lynch"—he refused to call him Master—"is done trying to get you?"

"He's never had more than one live-in at a time. So, yes, I think he's accepted that I'm never going to be his. That we're done. He doesn't even want to talk with me but has his lawyer handling things."

"That's good." Mason corrected himself, "No, that's great! No more mister creepy. Wait. So this Amber person's happy about it. Really?"

"Believe me. The girls are always thrilled. It's just me that didn't want it."

"Good." Mason finished off his beer, feeling satisfied, until he remembered something else. "You said he brands them with a new name."

"Yes, mine would have been Bastet after the Egyptian—"

"Please tell me that's just a figure of speech?" She looked confused, so he clarified. "Please tell me you didn't almost let that maniac burn a brand onto your skin like livestock?"

"No, silly. It's…" Cat laughed riotously, while Mason watched and waited. Finally she caught her breath, wiping the glee from her eyes. "No, sweet guy, this isn't the middle ages. Master Lynch just engraves their new slave name on a metal plate locked around their neck. That's all." She resumed chuckling, as if *he*, Mason, were the absurd one.

The loitering elephant smirked at him and at his dilemma. Cat thought women wearing dog collars on their necks and acting like slaves was normal and he…didn't.

An hour later, after a quick bit of fun in her attic, Mason drove them to town for dinner. He realized that at some point they'd need to talk about the whole BDSM thing, but he was happy to let it go for now. Especially since it seemed that Cat wasn't growing bored with vanilla sex. Not based on the way she'd climaxed earlier, shattering and shrieking for long minutes. Twice! Perhaps they should make use of the Burgundy Rose after all, just for the soundproofing, because the smirks on the guests' faces hanging out on the porch when they left suggested they'd heard it all.

"Why are you grinning like that?" Cat asked as Mason turned the car onto Main Street.

"No reason. Just wondering if you have any spare gags in the main house?"

Cat punched him in the arm. "I'm not that loud."

"Yes, you are," he countered, chuckling. "You screeched like a feral kitty-cat in heat." She shrieked in indignation, and Mason quickly added, "But I liked it! Believe me, Miss Sexy, there isn't anything you do in bed that I don't love."

"Is that true?"

"If our last round hadn't made me so damn hungry for food, I'd be turning the truck around right now just from this conversation. I can't get enough of you. No how, no way. I want you all the time."

Cat seemed reassured, but Mason wondered how long it would be before she'd had enough of boring old vanilla…and boring old him.

Chapter 11

~ her new Dom

Cat heard a car coming down the drive and ran outside. Her heart felt way too big for her chest. Mason's amazing gift had done that to her. Seeing his familiar pickup made her pulse race as fast as her feet.

"Thank you so much for all the tulips!" she cried, meeting him at the door to his truck.

Beaming, she threw herself into his arms the second his work boots hit the pavement. Pleasure, like a warm, soft blanket on a cold day, enveloped her as his strong arms came around to hold her tight against his body. She nestled against his chest, breathing in his familiar scent. It was delicious. He was delicious, and that familiar tingle started anew. Hard to believe they'd been having sex almost daily for a month, and she hadn't grown bored with the vanilla taste. Maybe she wouldn't ever. Maybe she just needed the *right* man.

Tilting her head up, she rested her chin on his hard chest and met his smiling eyes. "That was the most amazing thing anyone has ever done for me. I've vases and vases of beautiful spring tulips in every color imaginable. They're everywhere. How in the world did you get tulips in December?"

Mason looked fondly down at her. "Where there's a will, there's a way, as they say." He pulled her tight against him and kissed her silly.

"Come inside. I want to show them to you." She pulled free to grab his hand, and he let her tug him inside. "I could hardly believe it when the delivery van showed up and the guy just kept bringing in more and more bouquets. It was unbelievable." She swept her arms wide to encompass the red, yellow, purple, white, and pink blooms in vases, glasses, and bowls on every surface throughout her first floor.

"I'm glad you like them."

"Like them! They're my favorite flower. How'd you know?"

"You mentioned being here once in the spring and loving all the tulips. I decided you shouldn't have to wait until spring."

"Come on." Cat tugged his hand and turned toward the master bedroom. "The B&B is empty tonight, so come and let me thank you properly."

"No, wait. We need to talk."

His serious tone made her stop. She turned back to look at him, not liking the tight press of his lips and hint of worry in his narrowed eyes. Her stomach lurched—maybe her boredom wasn't the thing she should be concerned about. Had *he* tired of *her*? Was the incredibly generous gift Mason's way of saying thank you and sayonara? Gifts were certainly the way that Lynch dumped his girls. "Uh, okay. Is something wrong?"

Mason didn't reassure her. Instead he pulled her gently into the parlor and indicated the settee. "Sit," he ordered firmly.

Without a second's thought, she sat, the training hard to overcome, but Cat moved to rise again. The sharp aim of his finger and stern tightening of his eyes kept her in place. She didn't chafe at it, however. It felt right obeying a dominant guy. Always had. The only difference was Mason—had he always had such command under his sweetly considerate nature?

Cat's confusion and worry made her palms sweat. Her stomach churned as if she'd eaten rotten food for lunch.

It didn't help that Mason remained standing.

"I think we need to address the elephant in the room, so to speak." He paced away from her. "Or more accurately, the submissive in the room. It's a subject we've avoided over the last two months."

Cat startled. He was talking about her. It made her want to run to him, and it took all her willpower to remain where he obviously wanted her…with an entire room between them.

"I'm no longer Master Lynch's sub. I don't want to have anything to do with him." Did he not believe her?

"I know, and good riddance. I was extremely angry when I learned that Lynch abused you, and then to learn that you liked it." Mason's severe tone was knife-sharp, slashing her nerves and making her sick inside.

She shook her head vigorously, but didn't interrupt while he took a deep breath, clearly trying to calm himself. Cat's need to go to him, throw her arms around his stiff frame and reassure him was practically a physical thing. Fighting the yearning took all her energy.

At last, Mason came to her side. He sat next to her and grasped her hands in his strong ones. "I'm still sorry for the things I said and the way I left that day. It was a shock and I didn't understand and…" His head dropped and he repeated, "I really am sorry."

"It's okay. I know it was a shock. You've shown me over and over how much you care for me, and I—" Cat bit down on the words that would let him know just how very much she cared for him. It was too soon. They were too new. She was too new at being normal in the bedroom.

"I do care for you, but there's more to it than that."

She could see that he was still worried, and her stomach lurched all over again. Cat waited quietly for him to continue. The training again.

Mason cleared his throat and took a deep breath. "We haven't discussed any of it." He gestured broadly with his hands, suggesting something bigger, and then pointed toward the wine house that could be seen down the lane through the window. "You may have broken it off with Lynch, but you're still a submissive. I believe you still crave dominance in the bedroom. I worry that your sexual needs are not being met. That our sex isn't exciting enough."

Cat shook her head, disagreeing with him. She wouldn't lie. She'd always be a sexual submissive, but now she was more than that. Relief flooded her that this was his concern. "It's okay." She gave him a quick peck on the cheek. "Trust me. I've loved every scene…I mean, every time we've had sex. I haven't gotten bored at all."

"Not yet."

She opened her mouth to argue, but closed it at Mason's raised hand. It annoyed her, on some level, that she couldn't seem to stop the automatic response. *So what if subbing is still a part of me*, she argued with herself. *I can ignore that part.*

"Cat, come with me. I have a surprise for you. We're going to explore this side of you." He stood and offered his hand to her. She involuntarily leaned away, wondering what he meant. Mason thrust his hand closer, his expression stern, and she complied, placing her smaller one in his grip. Mason was different somehow, exuding power, dominance, and control to a degree she hadn't seen before.

He led her out the door and started toward the dungeon. Peanut and Gringo perked up from their late afternoon naps the minute they'd emerged from the house and followed them down the lane.

"Wait," she exclaimed. "We can't go there. It's reserved for tonight. Some San Francisco Domme."

Mason kept walking, gently pulling her along. "I reserved it. Or rather the dominatrix that has been training me reserved it on my behalf. I wanted to surprise you."

There was nothing on this earth he could have said that would have surprised her more. "*Training? Dominatrix?* But—"

"Stop talking, *Fernball*. And stop resisting me, unless you want to start our…*scene* outside on the park bench with you over my lap? You thought I didn't notice your little slip, didn't you?"

Cat opened her mouth, but he interjected, "No, don't answer. I'm not ready for a public display. And anyway, I told you not to talk."

They were almost at the door, and he grinned at her. "This Dom stuff takes some getting used to. I may slip up sometimes. And just so you don't think this is all for you, I'll admit that I haven't stopped thinking about tying you up since I saw the inside of the new and improved Burgundy Rose. I may have been shocked initially, but as I said before it fueled some wicked fantasies."

Cat was dumfounded, off kilter…and totally *turned on.* Mason the dominant was hot! That Mason wanted to tie her up, even hotter.

Meow-za!

She wanted to question him, wanted to know what was going on, but Mason had threatened punishment.

Oh what the hell!

"What's going on? What do you mean, you reserved it?"

"Open the door, Cat."

She punched in the code, and he pushed the door open wide.

Two tail-wagging pooches rushed forward. "No. Peanut. Gringo. Out." Mason's commanding tone amazed her, almost more than how her dogs—*her dogs*—scrambled backwards in their haste to obey him.

"In we go." He gestured for her to enter.

"No, wait," he amended. Mason gave her a cheeky grin and proceeded inside ahead of her without a backward glance, assuming Cat would follow docilely.

She did, of course. Incredible excitement mixed with confusion had her pulse pounding and her palms moist.

"But I don't understand. You went to a *dominatrix?*" Cat tried not to think about how absolutely jealous she was at the thought of another woman touching Mason. A Domme was a professional, she reminded herself. That was different, though she still didn't like it.

Another shocking thought struck her as Cat watched him looking about the dungeon. "Do you want me to top you?"

He laughed, a big loud bark of merriment. "No fucking way, sweet thang. I'm not, nor will I ever be, a submissive."

Their eyes met and he stared her down, until she dropped her gaze to his feet.

"No, Sir, I don't think you are." She was elated to realize that, apparently, all the dominatrix had done was teach him about being a Dom. "So you just went for train—"

"Because you keep talking when I asked for silence, I must assume that you *want* a spanking."

"What I want is an explanation." Cat couldn't seem to keep her mouth shut. However, she doubted he'd go through with it anyway. The delicious clenching deep in her core told her she'd like it very much if he did.

"A trade then." Mason's newfound mastery seemed to overwhelm the space as he walked around shutting and locking the door, closing the curtains, switching on the lights, and adjusting a chair here or a table there. "A trade," he repeated, not looking her way while he scanned the wall of crops and floggers. "Answers you'll get…*after* you get a much needed, long denied, spanking."

Kinky lust spread like flickering flames up her body. She felt hot, dizzy, hungry. And compliant. She'd happily do just about anything he asked. All the questions about why, when, and what was going on ceased to matter as her innate sexuality slipped out from where she'd stuffed it.

Barely audibly, she breathed, "Yes, Sir." She waited for instructions.

Rooted to her spot by the door, Cat watched as he continued to walk around and inspect everything, but this time it wasn't with shock on his face, rather more like contemplation, a small grin turning the corners of his lips as he occasionally ran his fingers across the different textures. Leather. Metal. Bamboo.

She shuddered, but didn't pretend to herself it had anything to do with dread.

"Here, I think." Mason patted the spanking bench. He had a black leather paddle in his hands, tossing it back and forth as if testing its weight, then smacking his hand with it. The sound cracked loudly in the quiet room and Cat jumped.

Only then did she see Mason's new dominance waver. "I'll never hurt you, Cat. Not like Lynch." Faltering a bit. "You know that…right?"

Cat weighed what she already knew about him in the face of this brand-new version. Mason had proven over and over that he cared about her. Proven that she could trust him. Proven that he was a great lover. Now, completely unexpectedly, Mason was showing her that he had it in him to be a dominant, and a great one, she sensed. Cat didn't know why or how he'd trained, but she knew that the dominatrix who had reserved Burgundy Rose was renowned in San Francisco. She suddenly understood that those 'work' trips to the city were for a vastly different kind of business—kinky business.

She glanced at Mason and he nodded encouragingly, but he didn't press her, the paddle now dangling quietly from his hand.

And then, best of all, Cat realized the most important thing about this startling development. Mason had done it all for her, to please her. *Just* for her. He may have said otherwise, but she knew he'd made the effort so they could share this other side of her sexuality.

Cat smiled, a bright, beaming happiness that she could feel shining brightly—just for him. She wanted desperately to tell

Mason how much she loved him, throw herself at him, and kiss him senseless.

Instead, she dropped her eyes respectfully down, before murmuring in her most kittenish timbre, "Yes, Sir. I trust you completely. I was a bad girl and ignored your direction to keep quiet. I await your correction."

Mason groaned. "God, that's hot!"

She tried to wipe the anything-but-repentant glee from her face, look contrite, but it was a lost cause—she was too thrilled, too aroused, and too absolutely eager to become his plaything. With Mason, she knew it would be her kind of kink, all the play and none of the drama. She almost giggled in her excitement, clenching her mouth to stop the joy from spilling out.

She risked glancing up at him through her lashes and their eyes met. Mason appeared to be fully cognizant of her mood. "Well okay, then." He winked. Their gazes still locked, he purposely slammed the paddle down hard on the leather bench, ensuring an explosive crack rent the air.

Cat tried hard not to react, but giddy with excitement and tingling with need, she trembled visibly. This time, Mason didn't falter. He walked to the red wingback throne and sat. "Kitty Cat, come stand before me and strip. Slowly."

Suddenly, she was reluctant, like a recalcitrant child that wanted to run away from punishment. Not afraid, exactly, but finding it hard to step forward. If she were a real cat, her tail would be between her legs.

It was the roleplaying of a D/s scene, of course, that affected her. The debasing situation reinforcing their differing positions—him, fully dressed and lording over her, and she, soon to be naked and kneeling. It was designed to make her subservience and submission real in *that* moment. To make real Cat's loss of power over her own body and over any pleasure or pain she would receive.

Trembling, her knees weak, Cat forced herself forward, her gaze on his feet. It was absurd, she acknowledged, because Mason now knew her naked body probably as well as his own, but she grew timid about removing her clothes at his command. She kicked off her shoes first—that was easy—and bent down to remove her socks. Hands shaking, she took off her top and then her jeans, shimmying them down over her hips and stepping out of them. She paused, hoping this would be enough. He could spank her plenty in her underwear. She flicked her eyes up for a second.

Mason's eyes were eating her up. That was a reward, in itself. The large bulge in his pants reassured her that he was just as affected by their play. "I believe I told you to strip." His strict tone made clear he'd brook no half-hearted compliance.

Cat jumped, quickly reaching behind her back to grope at the bra's clasp.

What's the big deal? She'd been naked wearing just a collar before entire parties of men.

But their game was so unexpected and so fresh. It felt like she was a brand new sub going through the gauntlet for the first time. It was as thrilling as it was unnerving. When her fumbling fingers couldn't seem to undo the hook, she ripped it over her head, her breasts bouncing free. She liked very much the harsh sound of his indrawn breath, and jiggled her boobs again for added effect. Then, finally, she pushed down her panties to stand naked before him.

"Very nice."

Pleasure suffused her. Pride in her hard-earned, tight body.

"Kneel."

Just like that, Cat was propelled back to her special place, the emotional state that aroused her like nothing else. She lowered herself elegantly, calling on her many hours of training, and assumed the presentation pose—ass on heels, hands on thighs that were spread wide, breasts proudly thrust forward, and shoulders back. Lowering her gaze was harder, the perverse desire to challenge him with a heated look rousing her sensibilities.

"I want to fuck you so hard." Mason groaned, the sound thick with lust. "But we have unfinished business. Regarding Mistress Cassandra, I want you to know that she was more of a consultant than anything else. There was no sex. I've also been reading up on BDSM, but this kink stuff is brand new to me. If I make a mistake, you have my permission to let me know. This has to be fun for both of us. Do you promise me you'll keep your boundaries intact?"

"Yes, Sir. Thank you, Sir." Everything Mason said filled her with gratitude and pleasure. He'd done all this for her, but he really wanted it, too. That made it one hundred percent better.

"Your safe words will be Miss Kitty and Fernball, for slow down and stop, in that order."

She snorted with laughter, unable to stop it. "You're kidding, right? You really want me to yell out, *Miss Kitty! Miss Kitty!* when I'm approaching my limits? I'll be laughing too hard."

"I'm not amused."

"Oh."

"I said you could correct my mistakes but these phrases fit the requirements of a safe word, unless you anticipate screaming Fernball while you climax?"

"Um, no. Sorry, Sir." She dropped her head in defeat. It seemed he'd already learned the intricacies of playing with a sub's headspace. She shivered. *God, he was good.* His manipulations were already working their magic on her.

"Catriona, tell me how you feel right now. Are you aroused?"

Her face shot up in surprise, her eyes searching for confirmation that he was serious. Mason stared, fixated, at her pussy, and her thighs quaked with the need to close before the onslaught of his intense inspection. Her sex clenched, pulsed, making her feel wet and oozy. Stunned, Cat realized that she might actually climax from the stimulation of his gaze alone. Had she thought him good at this play? He was magnificent! Never before had a Dom brought her so close to the edge without a single physical touch.

"I'm waiting."

Oh no! No, no, no! She wasn't normally a dripper, but she felt it. A drop of her juices was sliding out, tickling her labia, before falling to the floor. Cat felt an embarrassed blush rush up her chest to flame her face.

Mason jerked forward, leaning down to squint at the slate floor under her spread thighs, before zeroing in on her soaking pussy. As if in a daze, she saw a slow grin of satisfaction turn the corners of his lips as his eyes travelled unhurriedly up her body. They paused at her bosom to observe the rise and fall of her breasts as she drew in ragged breaths. Her already peaked nipples tightened sharply, sending a jolt of electricity to her core. Cat swayed, almost unable to keep upright, the desire turning her molten. She moaned, a guttural sound that was loud in the quiet room.

"Catriona, I expect you to answer my simple question. You'll stay on your knees until you do."

Her face felt hotter. Redder. Mortified that Mason could so easily transform her into a sex-mad slut. "Sir…I…um." She dropped her gaze to the floor.

"I want to see your eyes."

She shuddered, the delicious tingling travelling down her spine, spiking her lust. With great effort, she met his penetrating gaze. "Yes, Sir. I am aroused, Sir."

"I'm aware of that." He grinned, flicking his eyes to the growing wet spot on the floor. "Give me more."

"I…um…feel a great need to touch you and for you to touch me."

"Where and how do you want me to touch you? Don't leave anything out."

Mason was doing a major head-trip on her, expecting her not just to admit her need but lay it out in lurid detail for his perusal. Spread her need as widely as she was spreading her thighs. But Cat couldn't deny what it was doing to her, firing her like some phantasmagorical aphrodisiac.

Maintaining eye contact as Mason had ordered, she murmured, slow at first but picking up speed, "On my pussy, Sir. I want you to fondle me there, slip your fingers inside. I want you to suck my tits, bite them. Hard. I want you to fuck me…harder than ever before. I want to serve you. Suck you. Ride you. Submit to you in whatever way you desire. I…*please,*

Sir!" Her voice had increased in pitch till it was almost a wail. "I want you so badly."

"And you'll have me," Mason rejoined.

Laughing, he jumped to his feet and down from the dais. From the corner of her eye, she watched him merrily lope to the massive four-poster steel bed, pulling his shirt off as he went. Continuing to undress, removing his shoes and socks, he added, "But first, the promised spanking."

Cat was halfway to subspace and still he hadn't touched her. Kneeling on the cold stone floor, she shivered uncontrollably. But it wasn't from cold. Her body was hot all over. She sweltered with fiery desire, growing more aroused and wet by the minute.

"Come here, Catriona."

Finally. Breathing heavily, she climbed to her feet. Cat started toward Mason, fighting the urge to run and throw herself at him. She kept her eyes glued to the floor, unable to meet his knowing gaze. She had never felt so vulnerable in her life, having laid out her fawning desires before him for his gratification.

Reaching the bed, she waited before him in the attention pose, feet slightly apart, shoulders back, and hands clasped behind her. Cat held her chin high, but her eyes were downcast.

She heard Mason groan, a guttural lust-filled sound. He touched one finger to her chin and dropped it to her chest, trailing it down her front. "Stunning."

"Come." He stepped backwards to sit on the edge of the bed and she followed. "Lay across my lap, Catriona. Grasp my ankle with your hands and open your legs as much as possible in that position."

Mason seemed to know exactly what he wanted, and Cat wondered how long he'd planned this. She climbed onto him. He still wore his jeans and they felt rough against her belly. She hung over him, head almost to the floor with her naked ass high in the air.

"We're new in this, and I don't know your tolerance levels. So, remind me of your safe words."

Cat barely stopped her snort at his nonsensical choices. "Fernball and Miss Kitty, *Sir!*" She didn't manage to stop the trace of derision from slipping out at the end.

Smack!

"Ouch!" she cried. A round flame burned one ass cheek, but really Cat was more surprised than hurt by the unexpected swat.

"That was a bonus for the insolent tone, sweet Catriona. Will you be respectful in the future?"

"Yes, Sir."

Shit! Mason had certainly gotten his money's worth from his time with Mistress Whatever-her-name-was, and her backside was going to pay the price.

"Now, as I understand it, I should spell out your infractions and tell you what the punishment will be for each."

Shit! Shit! What have I done? It had been a mistake introducing Mr. Nice Town to wicked-city BDSM. But Cat knew she was fooling herself. She loved it. Every minute of it. Riding high on desire, she was this close to edging. All it would take was a little more.

As if Mason could read her thoughts, she felt his hand come to rest on her buttocks. He dutifully, rubbed the burn, following protocol, before fondling both mounds. Then...*yes,*

yes, yes…his hand slid down along the crevice between her cheeks until his fingers were between her parted thighs.

Cat squirmed. She tilted her ass higher and spread her thighs wider, as much as she could hanging over his lap. When his fingers finally found her wet cunt, a gruff rumbling moan escaped her lips, the sound more cat in heat than kitten's purr.

Mason chuckled, deep and low and amused. "Incredible. Watching your wet pussy drip." His voice was quiet but intense. "Tell me, is that a normal thing for you?" His fingers played with her juices, swirling the moisture around her folds, onto her thighs, and dipping inside her hole for more.

Cat whimpered, feeling her face flame all over again. "No, Sir. I've never done that before."

He laughed outright then, a delighted full-bellied chortle that rocked her on his lap.

"God, I adore you," Mason exclaimed. His declaration made her toes curl with excitement, as did the feel of his bulging erection pressing into her belly.

"It's time," he announced. "Four strikes each for talking out of turn, laughing at my choice of safe words, and not immediately answering my question."

"Oh!" She'd almost forgotten the reason she was hanging over him.

Smack! Smack! Smack! Smack!

Cat squealed, thrashing about on his lap. He alternated cheeks, but they weren't the light swats she'd expected from her newbie Dom. *They hurt!* She panted and fought the urge to let go of his ankle to rub her burning ass.

Smack! Smack! Smack! Smack!

"Aaack!" she shrieked. The second set had caught Cat by surprise. Where was the gentle rubbing? The time to get her wind back? She was too busy squealing and writhing to breath. Too busy concentrating on holding his ankle and not reaching for her fiery posterior to prepare for what was coming next.

Smack! Smack! Smack! Smack!

"Ouch! Ouch! Okay. Stop. *Fuuurn-ball!*" Cat wailed. It wasn't that the pain was unbearable, she'd endured much worse, but she couldn't catch her breath. She hadn't anticipated that Mason would have the skill or the desire to inflict the kind of pain that could take her to subspace, to that pleasure-pain plane where she floated on bliss. Next time she'd be prepared. Cat wouldn't underestimate him again.

"It's over. All done." Mason was laughing. "Was it too much, sweet thang?"

Cat continued to squirm and pant, her mind nearly overwhelmed by the eroticism of the experience. Her ass might feel hot but her pussy was on fire. She whimpered, not pain, but achy need driving her discomfort.

"Your concern might be more convincing," she pouted, "if you weren't laughing." He caressed her hot cheeks in soothing circles, and after a few minutes she ceased squirming and settled on his lap.

He kept chuckling, and finally she had to ask. "What's so funny, Mason?"

"You! You are one stupendous, sexy, brave, nutty, smutty, gorgeous sex-kitten. And, I adore you."

Cat liked the sound of that.

"I didn't expect to *ever* hear you utter that ridiculous safe word aloud, let alone in our first session. I'm feeling quite the manly man now."

Cat snorted. Opened her mouth to complain again, but then it was impossible.

Mason's exploring fingers were back in her sex. "So wet. Love it," he murmured. He flicked her clit, and she moaned and raised her pelvis higher.

"Shall we," Mason asked but it wasn't a question. Demonstrating a strength that Cat had learned to appreciate over the last two months, Mason easily picked her up off his lap like a rag doll. Standing with her in his arms, he rotated and tossed her onto the center the bed.

"I'm going to learn every trick this wicked bed can offer but right now I need to fuck you. On your back, subby," Mason ordered, while he unzipped his fly and shoved his jeans and briefs down in one rapid motion.

Cat's eyes locked onto his thick shaft. It stood out proudly from a nest of sandy brown hair. She rolled toward him. Mason stepped closer, and she hung off the bed's edge and reached out to touch him. She grasped his shaft with one hand and squeezed firmly, then slid her hand up and down his length. He was hot, hard, and velvety smooth. It made her hunger to taste him, and she reached out with her mouth to suck him inside. She fondled his balls and laved his dick and buried her face in him. Cat couldn't get enough of Mason. She loved the way he grunted and groaned, knowing it was because of what she was doing to him.

For a few minutes, Mason stood still and let her play. His hands tangled in her hair and caressed her face. "Enough. Get on your back and hold the rail at the headboard. Do not let go."

Cat scrambled to obey. Her hands latched onto the metal pipe. She craved the right to continue touching him, feel him everywhere, but she would keep her fingers locked in place until he released her. They'd never played like this before, but clearly Mason already understood that a verbal order would restrain her as securely as any rope or leather cuff.

He climbed over her. "You can talk now. I want to hear you when you come."

"Yes, Sir."

Cat opened her thighs wide for him, and Mason climbed between her legs. Grasping his dick he positioned it at her dripping sex. He pinned her with his eyes, and Cat couldn't have looked away for anything. She could see the driving lust there, and wondered if hers looked as wildly needy. Then he was pushing himself into her cunt, and she gasped. She could feel every hard, hot inch of him inside her. He filled her completely. Mason settled there for a long moment, his groin pressed to her mons.

Then, ever so slowly, inch by gradual inch, he pulled back out. He was moving at an agonizing crawl. Her entire body screamed for more, for glorious friction. She searched his face, and he grinned down wickedly, winking.

"Faster. Go faster," she urged.

Mason laughed. "You don't get to tell me what to do when we're here."

"Argh!" Cat moaned. Holding onto the railing with a death grip, she took the initiative and surged upwards with her pelvis, increasing the delicious friction. Then she dropped back to the bed.

Ahhh. That felt so good!

She surged again. Mason held himself rigidly stiff, giving her tacit approval. She slid up and down on him again and again. Each foray sent tingling jolts of pleasure through her, and she could think of nothing but the next surge. It was topping from the bottom, she supposed, but Mason's only order had been to hold the rail and she wasn't letting go. No way. She began to pulse on him at an ever-faster rate, and within seconds she was fucking Mason with everything she had. The look on his face told her it felt amazing to him, too.

"All right, Cat," Mason said. "You get your way, but it's going to cost you."

She gasped, but couldn't respond. Her mind ceased to function as Mason surged into her, taking back the power and claiming his right to bring her ecstasy. He pounded her over and over, giving her what she'd begged for, a hard, fast fucking.

Her eyes shut as everything in her world shrank to a bright pinpoint of approaching rapture. There was nothing but Mason's cock and her pussy, and the pleasure that was building and building and building.

Yes, her mind roared, and then she screamed it aloud, "Yes!"

She was so close, the very edge of bliss. Just a little more. Just a little harder. More thrust. She edged closer. The ache grew unbearable, her release tantalizingly out of reach. Unthinking, Cat grabbed his hips and yanked him down on her as she surged upwards.

"Yes! Mason!" she screamed and exploded in a white-hot shower of delight.

"Cat!" Mason shuddered and climaxed along with her.

She floated, weightless, for long endless moments in an ocean of euphoria, but she wasn't alone. Mason was there too, all around her, inside her. Her arms slid around to hold him tight as awareness returned. He was kissing her neck, trailing little gifts along her sensitized skin.

"Mmm. So good," she purred.

Mason rolled off her and collapsed next to her. Cat turned toward him and saw that he was grinning at her. "If I'd know it was this much fun, I'd have tried kink a long time ago."

Cat circled her finger through the damp curls on his chest and whispered, "It isn't always this great. Depends on who you're playing with."

"What did I say months ago…that we're made for each other. Inside or outside this dungeon, we're perfect together. Don't you agree…*Fernball?*"

Before she could answer, Mason leaned over and kissed her on the nose. Then on the lips. Then farther south to his two favorite little mountains.

Cat moaned. She wanted to give him a hard time about something but now couldn't remember what.

Mason rolled to the side and grabbed his cellphone, pressing buttons and flicking his finger across it. Turning back to her, he looked thoughtful. "I know it's early to bring this up. I want to train some more and really master some of this stuff, but Catriona Fern Morrison would you consider letting me collar you at some point in the future. Wear *this* here in the dungeon." He handed her his cell.

Cat took the phone and saw a photograph of a leather slave collar, the lovely aquamarine color matching her eyes. Simple. Classic. Beautiful. And best of all, it would be from Mason, her current boyfriend and her new Dom. And the one she wanted most in her future.

"Yes, I would that." She threw her arms around him and planted a quick kiss on his lips. "I can hardly wait until I can call you Master. Based on that scene, I don't think you're going to need too much more practice."

"Thank you." Mason kissed her back. "That means a lot to me...*Fernball.*"

"Would you stop! And, anyway, you can't use that nickname now that it's my safe word."

"Says who? You're still not likely to scream it out during a scene. I might, but that doesn't count, my sweet, fluffy, little *Fernball*"

"Ack. Stop! I demand you cease and desist." Laughing, Cat punched him hard in the shoulder, but clearly he had been practicing his Dom skills even more than she realized. Mason had her flipped over and across his lap in three moves.

Pinning her down with a hand, he landed a solid smack to her ass.

"Ouch!" she hollered, squirming but still laughing.

Mason chuckled, but she heard the authority loud and clear when he spoke. "Subs don't make demands. Subs follow orders. And subs don't top from the bottom, well at least mine won't repeat that mistake." He swatted her ass again. And again. And then he proceeded to rain down many little taps that burned twice as bright on her already red-hot rear. She panted and squirmed but couldn't get away from his playful assault.

"Okay, you win," she cried, laughing. "I cry uncle! I mean Fernball. Furnball. *Fuuuuurnball!*"

"Such a pretty bloomin' red," Mason chuckled. His hands rubbed the sting away.

Hanging over his lap, Cat laughed till tears came to her eyes. When she could finally catch her breath, she muttered, "I've created a monster."

"What did you call me?" he bellowed, but she could also hear humor in this tone.

"I said," she yelled back, "that I made a monster encouraging you to explore BDSM."

His hand slid between her thighs, and she sucked in a breath at the luscious feel of his fingers fondling her wet pussy. Feeling his growing erection pressing against her belly, Cat squirmed some more, just to tease him.

Mason leaned and whispered into her ear, "This monster's ready to play with his Lady Frankenstein." He sounded husky and hoarse and like a barely-leashed beast.

She moaned when he found her clit and flicked it. Cat tried to push up so she could turn to him, but his hand on her back kept her firmly in place.

"If I can't spank you into obedience, then I'll have to make you so hot and horny and desperate, you'll promise me anything."

She whimpered, her body already on overdrive.

Mason laughed, but kept his torment going until she mindlessly writhed and begged. "Please, Mason, I want you."

"Say that again and call me Master, my sweet, sexy *Fernball.*"

This time, Cat's compliance was immediate. "Please, Master! Call me anything you want, but please, please, please, fuck me silly."

Raw masculine gratification surged through Mason at her obedience and her rampant lust for him. Joy too, that she would soon wear his collar and later, he hoped, his ring on her finger.

Within seconds, Cat was flipped to her back, and he was inside her and they were fucking each other silly.

And it was a good thing the Burgundy Rose was soundproof, because Mason's roar of satisfaction thundered through the dungeon.

Set the dogs to barking outside.

And made Catriona Fern Fernball Morrison scream with rapturous delight.

— The end. —

Dear Reader,

Thank you so much for reading my book. If you enjoyed it, won't you please take a moment to leave me a review on Goodreads, Amazon, or your favorite retailer? And I hope to meet you sometime soon at a book signing or conference!

With thanks,

Kate

TURN THE PAGE FOR AN EXCERPT FROM KATE'S LATEST RELEASE FROM ENTANGLED PUBLISHING:

Her Gentleman Dom

Her Gentleman Dom

- excerpt -

...

Finn was stunned.

The blow to his psyche couldn't have been more shocking, even if she had shouted the words at him. It struck him like a punch to the gut. And to his ego. By holding himself in check, holding in his need to tie her up and do his dirty worst, he'd let them both down.

He stared at her beautiful face, averted from his gaze, whether because of embarrassment or disappointment, he didn't know. But his sweet bird had given them a precious gift.

"You are so brave. You amaze me. While I hold back, afraid of conflict, you push forward, giving us the chance for something great."

"What do you mean?" Her eyes searched his, but he wasn't ready to say more. It would be better to show her.

The smooth column of her neck enticed him. It was as if he could see her jugular pulsing with desire, and he hungered. He lowered his mouth to taste the soft pale skin. There was a light tangy hint of salt, but the texture was rich, warm silk. He kissed a trail along the curve of her neck toward her ear.

Lilli moaned, the sound as silky as her sweet skin.

Finn's inner demons wanted more, and before he thought too much about it, he bit her, a sharp nip to spark the sensitive nerves there. Lilli whimpered, the sound not displeasure but arousal. She turned back toward him, her hands drifting to his shoulders.

"More," she whispered, and Finn hoped he'd been right about her all along.

She was his to awaken. His to control, if he also had the guts to risk losing her.

He grabbed both her hands and yanked them over her head, locking them in place within his strong grip. Finn dropped his body on top of Lilli and kissed her fiercely, completely overpowering her. He was brutal, ravaging her mouth and forcing his tongue deep inside.

Lilli stilled, seeming stunned into unresponsiveness.

Then she moaned again—deeper, fuller, louder. "Please," the one word guttural and hungry.

"Up," he ordered, his tone harsh, domineering, pulling back to his haunches.

Obediently, she sat. He pushed her gown off her shoulders and whipped off her bra, baring her chest. He urged her to lie back again. Finn focused on her beautiful breasts. Perky, rosy, peaked. The perfect handful, and perfect for his mouth. Out of the corner of his eyes, he could see her watching him as he lowered his head and took one tight bud between his lips. Sucking, slurping, squeezing it with his mouth.

Lilli arched into him. Head thrown back, she made little mewling sounds as she moved restlessly beneath him.

Her responsiveness enflamed Finn. He needed to see how far he could drive her, wanted it to be further than she'd ever before gone. Finn bit down sharply on the nipple in his mouth.

Her throaty shriek rent the room. It was surprise, perhaps shock, but also undeniably ravening need. She squirmed beneath him, her pelvis bucking into his crotch, even as she arched impossibly higher in a mindless attempt to thrust her nipple further into his mouth.

Quickly, Finn laved the wounded tip with his tongue, soothing the pinch he knew she must feel. A sense of immense power filled him, the Dom in him loving the game, the lover in him delighted at her natural receptiveness.

There was also wonder. She was giving him yet another gift—allowing herself to let go and experience this different sort of lovemaking. How far he could push her? No leather whips or wooden paddles, not yet, but he could give her an idea of what awaited, a taste of the heights that could be reached from pleasure through pain.

Finn moved to her other breast ready to repeat the process, and she froze...waiting for the sharp bite.

"That won't do." The Dom in him wanted to control her pleasure and her pain. "Up." Sliding off the bed, he pulled her to standing and swiftly removed her dress and shoes, but left her panties. She stood there unmoving, unsure, her eyes locked on his like a deer caught in a wolf's gaze. Finn didn't soothe with words. It wasn't his way. His subs learned patience.

Never breaking eye contact, capturing her wide-eyed, wild gaze with his lustful one, he kicked off his wingtips and yanked off his tux, leaving only his briefs. Finn sat on the edge of the bed, his smile dropping to her pussy about a foot from his face. She trembled but didn't back away.

Infusing his voice with quiet authority, he threw down a gauntlet of obedience. "Take off your panties for me. Slowly."

She sucked in air, her uncontrollable gasp as sexy as any purred kitten-talk from an experienced sub. But Lilli didn't move, only the perceptible quivering of her belly, revealing that she was in flight-or-fight mode.

Finn tilted his head, studying in the baby blue lace decorating her sapphire panties. The delicate pattern trailed down her crotch, tantalizing him with glimpses of her sex. He cleared his throat but didn't look up.

Moving as if it took great effort, Lilli lifted her hands and hooked her fingers into the elastic band around her hips. He could feel her eyes boring into him but kept his focus on her sex. She needed to learn that Doms didn't encourage compliance, they expected it.

With the ease of a Lothario, he crossed his arms over his briefs. His cock jutted like a longsword, but he couldn't let her see how much she affected him. Doms controlled everything— their sub's physical responses and their own.

Finn waited. Would she yank them off in hasty mortification or follow his instructions? It was way too soon for training, for punishment, but she would have to learn obedience if she was to become his. Then, slowly—whether from mortified hesitation or willing compliance, he couldn't gage—Lilli pulled down her panties. He hungered for every tantalizing inch of skin she revealed as the scrap of satin lowered. He leaned closer, just inches from her crotch, where her panties were taut around her thighs. His mouth watered as he stared at her sex.

He grunted, "Very pretty."

…

Her Gentleman Dom

PUBLICATION DATE - 10/15/18

AVAILABLE IN PRINT & EBOOK FROM AMAZON

Other books by Kate Allure

Bed & Breakfast & Bondage 2

Her Gentleman Dom

Lawyer Up

Laying Pipe

Playing Doctor

Subscribe to Kate's Newsletter at:

www.kateallure.com

Twitter: @KateAllure

Facebook.com/KateAllure.Sizzling.Romance

Pinterest.com/KateAllure

https://www.instagram.com/kate.allure

Acknowledgements

Thank you to all who helped with this novel. First, I must thank my sweet, sexy, and supportive graphic designer (who also happens to be my husband) as well as my close friends, critique partner Anna and proofreader extraordinaire Sandy. As always, I'm grateful for the encouragement of my agent Louise Fury of The Bent Agency. I also offer a shout out to family and friends for their support and, most importantly, to all of you who took the time to read this novel. I'm thankful and hope that you enjoyed it!

About the Author

Kate Allure writes erotic romances that celebrate sensuality, sexual exploration and, of course, true love. Writing for Entangled Publishing and Sourcebooks, her books feature real women meeting handsome professional, working men as they go about their everyday lives—and the fun they have behind closed doors! Her work is "Escapism of the richest, most decadent variety," 4 Stars (*RT Book Reviews*), and "sizzling and sensual. Intense chemistry, great characterization, and a kinky page-singeing ending will have readers clamoring for more," (*Publishers Weekly*). Kate's non-fiction writing included working for American Ballet Theatre and New York City Ballet, and recently creating the *Romance Readers Guide to Historic London* under the name Sonja Rouillard. Beyond writing, Kate's passions include traveling and exploring all things sensual with her loving husband.

BDSM disclaimer for my readers ~

You've all seen the silly TV ads where a racecar driver performs some stunt and at the bottom it reads, "Professional driver, closed course—Do Not Attempt." This is that…do not try this stuff at home. Do not try the BDSM acts in my stories unless you know what you're doing, have a safe partner, and take responsibility for your actions. Specifically, B&B&B is a fictional story that explores BDSM and the practices inherent in the lifestyle. It is not intended to be a how-to manual or advocate that anyone try anything described here. This author and publisher take no legal responsibility for any results of anyone attempting to copy the sexual acts depicted in the story. Lastly, I believe wholeheartedly that everyone should follow the SSC code—Safe, Sane, and Consensual.